Justin D'Ath has built cars, picked fruit,
mined for iron, worked in a sugar mill, studied to be a priest
and drawn cartoon strips. He has written several books for
children including *Why did the Chykkan cross the galaxy?*
and *Sniwt.* He teaches professional writing and editing,
and lives in Spring Gully, Victoria.

This book is for
Elizabeth, Erin and Elly.

First published in 2000 by
Allen & Unwin
9 Atchison Street
St Leonards NSW 1590
Australia
Phone: (61 2) 8425 0100
Fax: (61 2) 9906 2218
E-mail: frontdesk@allen-unwin.com.au
Web: http://www.allen-unwin.com.au

National Library of Australia
Cataloguing-in-Publication entry:

D'Ath, Justin.
The upside-down girl.

ISBN 1 86508 134 5.

I. Denton, Terry, 1950-. II. Title.

A823.3

Designed and typeset in Rotis Sans Serif 11pt by Sandra Nobes
Printed in Australia by Australian Print Group

2 4 6 8 10 9 7 5 3 1

THE

A gravity-defying

UPSIDE-DOWN

adventure by

GIRL

Justin D'Ath

Pictures by
Terry Denton

ALLEN & UNWIN

17 A chapter from later in the book (but you can read it first if you like)

'Gravity works like a giant magnet,' explained the physicist, a guest on the popular TV show, 'Famous People'. 'It pulls everything towards the centre of the earth.'

'So why not me?' asked the other guest, a small, dark-haired girl who appeared to be suspended upside down from the studio ceiling.

'Repeated exposure to electromagnetic forces, along with the reverse Gs every time the car descended, seem to have de-gravitised you.'

Martin Beam, host of the show, interrupted. 'If she was simply de-gravitised, wouldn't she weigh nothing? I mean, look at her,' – he jerked his thumb upwards – 'she weighs *less* than nothing!'

Both men peered up at the girl on the ceiling.

'Since gravity is no longer holding her down,' explained the physicist, 'the centrifugal forces caused by the earth's rotation are actually pushing her away from its centre. So instead of falling down, she falls[1] *up*!'

'Can she be fixed?' asked Martin Beam.

'I don't know,' the physicist admitted. 'This is the very first case of it ever recorded. You've made history, Miss...um...'

'Hu,' said the upside-down girl.

'Who?'

'That's right.'

The physicist looked puzzled.

'H-U,' she spelled.

'Bless you!' he said.

---

[1] The proper word is llaf. You fall down, but you llaf up.

The upside-down girl rolled her eyes towards the floor. 'I was *spelling* it.'

'Spelling what?' he asked.

'Her name,' said Martin Beam.

'What is it?' asked the physicist.

'Hu.'

The physicist pointed upwards. 'Her.'

1 The real start of the book (or: Brittany's dream[2])

Brittany's kindergarten class were asked to draw pictures of themselves as grown-ups. The other children drew veterinarians, firefighters, flight attendants and astronauts; Brittany drew a circle of reporters and photographers all crowded round a slim, dark-haired woman with a huge, red-crayon smile.

'Which one is you?' asked the teacher.

'The lady in the middle.'

'Look everybody!' Mrs Donato said as she hung Brittany's drawing alongside the others on the classroom wall. 'Brittany is going to be a film star.'

'No, I'm not,' said Brittany.

'A singer?'

Brittany shook her head.

'A model?'

'Nope.'

Mrs Donato smiled. 'I give up. What *are* you going to be, Brittany?'

'Famous!'

That was her dream. One day the whole world would know the name 'Brittany Hu'.

---

[2] Not to be confused with Brittany's Dream, a pigeon you'll meet in Chapter 120.

2 Brittany who? (or: Twenty ways not to become famous)

It had seemed simple enough when she was four. But as she grew older, Brittany came to realise that becoming famous was tricky. It wasn't like other careers – there weren't any courses you could study or training you could do to make you famous. In fact, if you wanted to be famous you had to do something else first – usually something sporty or artistic – and be really, *really* good at it. Or you could become Prime Minister, fly to the moon, or make an important discovery such as a new comet or the cure for a disease.

Over the next few years Brittany tried all sorts of things: oil painting, ballet, BMX racing, even singing (until her mother put a limit on how long she could stay in the shower).

She took up long-distance swimming but gave it up after swallowing a jellyfish.

She came 2852nd in a Fun Run.

She learned the recorder, the piano, she took violin lessons. She even practised playing her grandfather's bag-pipes every day after school (until Mr Rankin, next door, offered her $2 a day to stop).

She asked her little brother to teach her chess, but he kept beating her.

She joined a pony club and broke her collarbone.

She went in a karate competition and dislocated her little finger.

She had a go at pole vaulting, but instead of landing on the inflatable mattress she'd set up on the lawn, Brittany sailed across the side fence and dented Mr Rankin's brand new Harley Davidson motorcycle. (*It* dented her shoulder.)

During one of her stays in hospital, Brittany wrote a novel that filled two whole exercise books. One of the friendly nurses posted it off to a publisher for her. The publisher sent it back two weeks later with a note to Brittany saying she had lovely handwriting, but a man called Lewis Carroll had already written a book all about Alice's adventures in Wonderland. (Can't publishers *read*? In Brittany's book it was *Downunderland*!)

She tried out for Dorothy in her school's production of *The Wizard of Oz* and was given the part of a munchkin.

She campaigned to be school captain but nobody – not even Morgan Barker, her best friend – voted for her.

She wrote to NASA about becoming the first kid in space and they wrote back and said 'wait till you grow up'. ('How can I be the first *kid* in space when I'm grown up?' she wondered.)

She lost hours of sleep searching the night sky, but the only comet she discovered turned out to be a moth having a snooze on the other end of the telescope.

She nearly made herself throw up experimenting with horrible-tasting ways of getting rid of those little bumps on your tongue.

Nothing worked. Here she was almost starting high school and people still said, 'Brittany who?'

3 Simple!

Amazingly, it was her brother who provided the answer. Lukas was nine and a bit of a pain, but for her birthday that year he gave Brittany the book that was to change her life. As soon as she opened it, Brittany knew how she was going to become famous.

She would set a new World Record!

The book was the *McGuinness Book of Records* and it was full of people who had become famous for doing really kooky things.

A Scotsman, for example, had walked right around the British Isles backwards. In Holland a woman had knitted a pair of gloves with 488 fingers. And a boy in Canada had taken 215 consecutive rides on a roller-coaster.

Brittany wondered how many times the Scotsman had tripped over. She tried to estimate how long it took the person the Dutch woman had knitted the gloves for to paint their fingernails. But it was the roller-coaster record that really interested her. Brittany's family lived right near the centre of Sydilly, only a few kilometres from Loony Park, the biggest fun park in the country. All she had to do was take 216 consecutive rides on the Loony Park roller-coaster and she would be famous. Simple!

4 Well, not quite so simple

On the Saturday after her birthday, Brittany and her brother caught the bus to Loony Park. She took Lukas along as her Official Witness. If you were setting a World Record, it said in the book, you had to have someone watching. To make sure you didn't cheat, Brittany supposed. And to count how many times you did whatever it was you were doing, or to time how long you did it for.

Lukas had a pad and a pen to mark down the number of rides she took. He'd brought along his camera as well, so there would be photographic evidence of her record-breaking performance.

'A photo of you chucking up!' he said gleefully.

'I'm not going to chuck,' said Brittany. She hoped not, anyway (and had skipped breakfast, just in case). 'But maybe you'd better take the photo at the start – before my hair gets messed up.'

Lukas poked the camera in her face. 'Say cheese...'

'Not yet, Lu–!'

Flash!

'What did you do that for?' she asked crossly. 'We aren't even there yet!'

Lukas grinned. 'If you're going to be famous, you'll have to get used to it.'

Brittany tried to catch her reflection in the bus window. 'How do I look?'

'Sort of green.'

It was just hunger, Brittany told herself. She should have had breakfast. She should have... *stayed in bed*!

5 Let's kick but

ROLLER-COASTER CLOSED FOR RENOVATIONS

Brittany breathed a secret sigh of relief. 'What a shame! Oh well, I suppose we can come back another time.'

Lukas took a photo of the sign. 'Let's check out the other rides.'

'I'm not in the mood.'

'Don't you want to break a World Record?'

'Of course I do. But I've got to wait till they fix the roller-coaster, don't I.'

Her brother turned his camera on a nearby ride. 'The merry-go-round's still working.'

'So?' said Brittany.

'So you could set a new merry-go-round record.'

She hated having to admit it, but: 'Lukas, you're brilliant!'

Ripping open her backpack, Brittany dragged out the *McGuinness Book of Records*. 'M' for *Merry-go-round*... Bummer! A girl in Turkey had ridden one non-stop for three days. Three whole days! Loony Park was only open from ten in the morning until midnight, so breaking that particular record was impossible.

But there were lots of other rides at Loony Park...

They looked up *Ghost train* and discovered that a Frenchman had stayed on one for 42 hours.

What about the Octopus? 502 consecutive rides. (At three minutes a ride, with a minute for people to get on and off, that worked out to 33 hours.)

Ferris wheel – 51 hours.

Stingray – 800 rides (38 hours).

Dodgem cars – 2 days, 3 hours and 44 minutes.

Mad Mouse – 466 rides (23 hours).

'It's impossible!' Brittany said finally. 'We'd have to stay here for the whole *weekend* to break any of these records.'

'What about the Gravity Buster?' Lukas asked.

Brittany took a deep, slow breath. The Gravity Buster was the newest and scariest ride at Loony Park. She had never been on it. It was a big open-topped car that shot up the side of a 500-metre tower on a set of magnetic rails. The sign said it pulled a force of 5 G, which meant the car accelerated up the tower so fast that on the way up you weighed five times what you normally did (Brittany would weigh nearly 200 kilograms!). When it was nearly at the top, it slowed right down and stopped. But only for a moment – after about half a second, it plunged back down, backwards, at *minus* 5 G!

Just thinking about it was enough to make Brittany's stomach churn. Nervously, she looked up 'G' in the *McGuinness Book of Records. Glass balancing, Gobstopper spitting, Gumboot throwing.* There was definitely no *Gravity Buster.*

'Looks like we're in business!' said Lukas.

'How do you figure that out?' Brittany asked. 'There *isn't* a record for the Gravity Buster.'

'So start a *new* one!'

'I don't think you can do that.'

Lukas snatched the book away from her and flipped through to the back page. 'Look!' he pointed.

There was a special form for starting new records.

'Description of activity,' it said at the top. Using the pen he had brought along to keep a tally of her roller-coaster rides, Lukas wrote:

Gravitty buster

'That's too many Ts,' Brittany told him.

He scratched out one of them. **Gravitty buger**. 'Let's kick butt!'

Brittany was staring at what he'd written. 'Lukas, you're hopeless! It's the *double* T that's the problem.'

'Let's kick but,' he said.

6 Guinea pigs

'Why don't *you* do it?' Brittany asked as she and Lukas waited in the queue.

'I'm not the one who wants to be famous.'

'I think I've changed my mind.'

Lukas crinkled his nose dis-believingly. 'Don't lie! Becoming famous is all you ever talk about.'

Brittany wished she had kept her mouth shut. Shielding her eyes against the sun, she peered up at the enormous steel tower with its set of skinny railway tracks running all the way to the top. 'I'm scared of heights.'

'Don't worry, you won't be looking dow—'

His words were cut off by a shrieking siren. At least, that's what it sounded like at first. Then Brittany realised what it really was – people screaming! But it wasn't the fun-screaming that people made in ghost trains or on roller-coasters, this was *real screaming* – the sort of screaming you heard in movies when the escaped tyrannosaurus blundered into the crowded ballroom, or when the rubber raft full of preschoolers was swept over the 100-metre-high waterfall (with crocodiles waiting at the bottom).

There was a rumble. The ground trembled. Then out of its launching shed flashed the Gravity Buster. Covering the 200 metres to the base of the tower in the blink of an eye, it shot straight up the side. Brittany watched with a not-very-nice, bubbly feeling at the bottom of her stomach as it slowed, then stopped 500 metres above them. Five hundred metres – that was *half a kilometre!* It looked tiny up there, like a beetle clinging to the top of a stick. But of course it wasn't a beetle – it was a car. And there were *people* in it. Brittany could just make out the backs of their heads as they sat there, strapped in like guinea pigs in some kind of giant laboratory experiment. Then – *whoosh!* – down they came in a shrieking, heart-stopping blur and, just as quickly as they'd come out, disappeared back into the shed.

'See!' Lukas showed her his watch. 'Up and back in fifteen seconds. You'll be able to do 200 rides in no time.'

The bloodcurdling, we're-about-to-die screams still rang in Brittany's ears. 'Wh-who s-said anything about t-t-two hundred times?'

Lukas tapped her backpack where the *McGuinness Book of Records* made a hard, rectangular bulge in the fabric. 'It would look pretty wussy: *Gravity Buster. Brittany Hu, of Australia. 5 consecutive rides.*'

'Do you think ten would be enough?'

'All the other records are for at least a hundred. Plus,' Lukas added knowledgeably, 'if you only did ten, someone would come along and break it the very next day.'

'You mean tomorrow?'

'No, not tomorrow! But as soon as they found out what the record was.'

Brittany sighed. She knew he was right. And if someone broke her World Record, she would stop being famous.

'Okay.' Her nails dug into her sweaty palms. 'T-two hu-hundred it is.'

'Now you're talking!' Burrowing into his back pocket, Lukas pulled out a small square of silver foil. 'Here, I've brought along a secret weapon.'

'What is it?'

'Carsick pills.'

'Isn't that cheating?'

'Suit yourself,' Lukas said.

There was another bloodcurdling shriek, another rumble. Seconds later, the Gravity Buster was way up at the top its tower, with another load of human guinea pigs screaming their lungs out.

Brittany fumbled to unwrap the silver foil. It contained eight small white pills. 'Do I take them all?'

'Two now, then two more every four hours.'

'Every four *hours*? No way am I staying in that thing for four hours!'

Her brother gripped her arm. 'Say to yourself: "I'm going to be famous."'

'I'm going to be famous,' Brittany whispered.

'Louder.'

'I'm going to be famous.'

'Louder.'

'I'M GOING TO BE FAMOUS!'

'Excellent,' said Lukas. 'Now take your pills.'

7 Another chapter about guinea pigs

Well, it isn't really about guinea pigs, it's about lemmings. Not lemons, lem*mings*. They're little animals that look a bit like guinea pigs. They live in the Northern Hemisphere, way up in the Arctic Circle where it's really cold. What's interesting about them is every so often they all rush down to the beach, jump in and swim out to sea. Which would be okay if they were good swimmers (or fish), but they aren't. So you can guess what happens.[3]

---

[3] Choose your own ending: (a) they get saved by friendly mermaids, (b) they dissolve and turn into a delicious fizzy drink called lemmingade, or (c) they drown.

You're probably wondering what this has got to do with the story. Read the next bit and find out.

8 The next bit

Brittany and Lukas's father was a scientist who worked in the noxious wildlife division of the CSIRO. His job was to find ways of controlling creatures that had been introduced into Australia and were harmful to the environment. His latest project was cane toads, and that's where lemmings come into the story.

Six months before Brittany's birthday (the one when Lukas gave her the *McGuinness Book of Records*), their father went to Norway to study lemmings. What he wanted to find out was *why* they swam out to sea like that. And he did find out: it was *lemmingitis*, a virus only lemmings could catch that made them think they were fish.

Mr Hu (really he was *Doctor* Hu, but he didn't call himself that because people made jokes about some old TV show) came back to his laboratory in Sydilly and changed the virus so that cane toads could catch it. The new virus was called *Bufo*[4] *lemmingitis* and it made cane toads think they were lemmings (which thought they were fish).

Bufo lemmingitis was extremely contagious. Within a few weeks of its release into the environment, not a single cane toad was left in Australia. They had all caught the virus, hopped down to the sea and swum away.

[4] *Bufo* comes from the Latin name for cane toads, *Bufo marinus.*

'Good riddance!' everyone thought. Cane toads were just about the worst pests ever brought into the country. Not only did they kill all sorts of native insects and fish and frogs, but they poisoned birds and cats and dogs if they (birds and cats and dogs) tried to eat them. And they were really yucky to stand on if you went outside at night without your shoes on.

Now, thanks to Brittany and Lukas's dad, all the cane toads had gone. Mr Hu was a national hero! He was…

9 Famous

What made Brittany spew (apart from stepping on cane toads, TV shows about eye operations, and finding half a cockroach when she was partway through eating a hamburger) was this: she had been trying all her life to be famous, and now her father had become famous without even trying.

10 The price of fame

'Four dollars fifty,' said the woman at the ticket window outside the Gravity Buster building.

'We've got All Day Passes,' Lukas said.

They showed her the ink-stamps on the backs of their hands and she let them go in.

11 Infamous

That's a word you might have to look up in the dictionary if you haven't read a book by that name. You'll need to know what it means later on.

12 Brittany Hu, human pancake

When her turn came to ride the Gravity Buster, Brittany climbed into the big open-topped car with eleven other scared-looking passengers. The car sat on its rails inside a short, low tunnel. Beyond the mouth of the tunnel, the sun glinted on the two thin silver strips of steel as they crossed the 200 metres of flat ground to the foot of the tower. Then they swooped sharply up – *straight up!* – and disappeared in the direction of the sky.

Two young men wearing Loony Park uniforms strapped everyone into their seats with a complicated system of buckles and harnesses. After they had double-checked that all the passengers were safely trussed up, the attendants disappeared into two control booths set well clear of the launching platform. A bell rang. A row of green lights started flashing.

This is it, Brittany thought. We're all going to die!

There was a deafening shriek. Actually, it was *twelve* deafening shrieks. Brittany didn't realise she was one of the shriekers until the Gravity Buster was out of the tunnel. In fact, everything happened so fast she didn't even know the car was moving until it was out of the tunnel.

A huge weight was pushing her backwards, squashing her into her seat – it was the 5 G force caused by the car's massive acceleration. By the time the Gravity Buster reached the foot of the tower, it was doing 350 km/h and Brittany knew what it felt like

to weigh nearly a quarter of a tonne (sort of like a pancake).
Then – *whoosh!* – up they went: up, up, up, way up into the
sky, straight up towards the blinding sun. Brittany was still
screaming – everyone was – but all she could hear was the
rushing of the wind which whipped the sound out of her
wide-open mouth and flung it away somewhere far behind
and below her. Then everything...

just...

stopped.

The car was vertical. Brittany and the other eleven passengers were lying on their backs, half a kilometre above the
ground, frozen with fear. All around them was sky. They
seemed to be hanging in space. Nobody was screaming now,
everybody was holding their breaths, waiting for the Gravity
Buster to...

They were falling. Down they went (all screaming
their lungs out again): down, down, down at 350 km/h.
BACKWARDS!

This time Brittany didn't feel all squashed and pancakey
like she had on the way up; now she felt light and sort of
balloony – as if she weighed *less* than the air that rushed up

past her. The harness cut into her stomach and shoulders, dragging her down, down, down with the car. If everyone hadn't been strapped so tightly into their seats, the Gravity Buster would have left her and the other eleven passengers behind, left them all hanging in the air like cartoon characters who had run off the edge of a cliff but hadn't started to fall yet. It was the weirdest feeling. And the scariest. But it didn't last long.

In the blink of an eye (well, 24 eyes, actually) the ride was over. They were back in the launching shed and the two attendants were descending from their control booths to unbuckle everyone.

'You can stop screaming now,' one of them told Brittany as he started to undo her harness.

Embarrassed, she clamped her mouth shut. But straight away she opened it again. 'Don't undo me!'

'I beg your pardon?' The attendant looked surprised. 'Usually people can't get out quickly enough!'

Brittany explained about her record attempt. The man listened doubtfully, then went away to talk to the other attendant. Meanwhile, the other eleven passengers had all climbed out and were walking shakily towards the exit. They looked like people in a science-fiction movie who had just been released from the aliens' flying saucer. Much to Brittany's surprise, she didn't feel too bad, just a little dizzy. Otherwise she was quite relaxed. It was probably the carsick pills. Despite Lukas's advice to take two every four hours, she had been so nervous about going on the Gravity Buster that she had taken all eight of them in one go. Now she hardly felt nervous at all. Just sleepy. She yawned.

The attendant came back. 'Okay. You can go for your record. But Loony Park takes no responsibility if anything happens to you. Nobody has ever ridden the Gravity Buster more than once before.'

'Excellent!' Brittany thought. She would definitely be setting a new World Record.

When she explained about Lukas acting as her Official Witness, one of the attendants helpfully found a chair for him and placed it over by the tunnel wall. Lukas sat down and opened his notebook.

At the top of the page he wrote: **1**.

13 Up there with the birds

On Brittany's second ride in the Gravity Buster, she hardly screamed at all.

After four rides she stopped screaming altogether. *She* stopped, the others didn't. A different eleven each time, eleven fresh sets of lungs – what a racket! Without all their noise the ride would have been quite enjoyable. *Whoosh! whoosh!*, up and down. It was mesmerising, rhythmical, almost relaxing. The best bit was at the very top of the tower, when the Gravity Buster hung motionless 500 metres above the ground. For those one or two seconds the other eleven passengers stopped screaming, there was no wind rushing past her ears, it was peaceful. All Brittany could hear was birdcalls. And the view was terrific.

On her eighth ride Brittany spotted her house in the distance. (It was quite easy to see because of Mr Rankin's tall, red-roofed pigeon house next door.)

On her tenth ride she began to notice how many birds were flying past. All sorts of birds – bright, noisy parrots, little twittering swallows, slow-flying hawks, whirring doves, flocks of ducks, solitary herons, green and yellow honeyeaters, tiny blue wrens, an owl – and all going in the same direction.

She even spotted a couple of emus crossing the road half a kilometre from the Loony Park entrance. Or perhaps she dreamed she saw them. Whoever heard of emus in the middle of Sydilly? Maybe all of it was a dream. (Was that a peacock down near the traffic lights?) Brittany yawned and blinked her eyes a few times. The pills were making her very drowsy.

Somewhere between her eighteenth and twentieth rides, Brittany lost track of things. All she wanted to do was... (Yawn!) She couldn't keep her eyes... (Yawn!) She felt so...

14 Sleeping on the job

'Wake up,' someone was saying.
A man's voice.

Brittany groaned and stretched.
She had been dreaming about an
awards ceremony. Leonardo DiCaprio
had been presenting her with the Best
Actress Oscar for her role in *Titanic 2*. She opened her eyes.

Bummer! It wasn't Leonardo DiCaprio. It was a man wearing a uniform that looked familiar. 'Loony Park' it said on the front of his T-shirt.

'Hullo, sleepyhead!' He smiled.

He wasn't one of the attendants she had seen before. 'Who are you?'

'Ben,' he said. 'I work the evening shift.'

Evening shift? Ben began undoing the first of the four large buckles that held her into her seat. 'Don't do that!' she cried.

'Why not?'

'I don't want to get out.'

'You have to,' he said. *Click!* went the second buckle. 'We're all going home now.'

'But I want to make a World Record!'

'Isn't twelve hours long enough for you?' asked Ben, undoing the third buckle.

Twelve hours? What was he talking about? Brittany peered towards the tunnel entrance and noticed something very peculiar – it was dark outside.

'Wha-what time is it?'

'Nearly midnight.'

Nearly midnight! 'Have I been in the Gravity Buster all this time?'

Ben nodded.

Then she'd done it! She'd set a World Record. 'How many rides did I do?'

'You'll have to ask your brother,' Ben said, reaching for the last buckle.

She glanced over at Lukas. There he was still sitting in his chair next to the tunnel wall. But something was wrong – his head was slumped forward on his chest, as if he was...

Asleep!!!

Her Official Witness was fast asleep!

'LU-U-U-U-K-A-A-A-AS!'

At the very moment Brittany screamed, Ben undid the final buckle.

15 Lukas woke up, or did he?

Lukas woke up when Brittany screamed. At least, he *thought* he woke up. Then he realised he must still be asleep. Because it's only in dreams that your sister can fly.

16 Upside down

'Oooow!' Brittany groaned.
She climbed groggily to her feet. The floor
seemed strange. It wasn't flat like a normal floor,
it curved upwards towards the walls. And it was
bumpy like corrugated iron. But, weirdest of all, it
had lights poking out of it. On long cords. Hanging *upwards*!
'Brit?' said her brother's voice.

'Lukas,' she growled, forgetting her bumps and bruises,
'how could you go to sleep? Now my record won't count! I
won't be famous.'

Lukas laughed, the little rat! Brittany looked round
angrily. Where was he? She looked left, she looked right, she
looked...up.

What on earth!!!?

Lukas and a whole crowd of people were standing
upside down on the ceiling! In the middle of the crowd, also
upside down, was the Gravity Buster. Several of the upside-
down people were pulling out their cameras and pointing
them down at her.

Her upside-down brother grinned. 'I don't think you have
to worry any more about not being famous,' he said, just as
the first camera flashed.

17 A chapter you've read before (but you can read it again if you like)

'Gravity works like a giant magnet,' explained the physicist,
a guest on the popular TV show, 'Famous People'. 'It pulls
everything towards the centre of the earth.'

'So why not me?' asked the other guest, a small, dark-haired girl who appeared to be suspended upside down from the studio ceiling.

'Repeated exposure to electromagnetic forces, along with the reverse Gs every time the car descended, seem to have de-gravitised you.'

Martin Beam, host of the show, interrupted. 'If she was simply de-gravitised, wouldn't she weigh nothing? I mean, look at her,' – he jerked his thumb upwards – 'she weighs *less* than nothing!'

Both men peered up at the girl on the ceiling.

'Since gravity is no longer holding her down,' explained the physicist, 'the centrifugal forces caused by the earth's rotation are actually pushing her away from its centre. So instead of falling down, she falls *up*!'

'Can she be fixed?' asked Martin Beam.

'I don't know,' the physicist admitted. 'This is the very first case of it ever recorded. You've made history, Miss...um...'

'Hu,' said the upside-down girl.

'Who?'

'That's right.'

The physicist looked puzzled.

'H-U,' she spelled.

'Bless you!' he said.

The upside-down girl rolled her eyes towards the floor. 'I was *spelling* it.'

'Spelling what?' he asked.

'Her name,' said Martin Beam.

'What is it?' asked the physicist.

'Hu.'

The physicist pointed upwards. 'Her.'

18 Problems with being de-gravitised: Problem #1 – drinking

'Her name is Brittany Hu,' explained Martin Beam. 'Spelt H-U.'

Slowly a look of understanding crossed the physicist's face. 'You mean like that famous doctor who got rid of all the cane toads?'

Martin beamed. 'He's her father, as a matter of fact. I had him on the show just last week.'

'Yes, I watched it,' said the physicist, looking suddenly more animated than he had during the entire interview. 'What a remarkable fellow!'

The host of 'Famous People' leaned sideways and spoke confidentially to his right-side-up guest. 'There's talk he might be getting a special award from the Prime Minister.'

'They ought to *make* him Prime Minister. Imagine using lemmings to solve the cane-toad problem!'

'Only he would have thought of it.' Martin Beam shook his head wonderingly. 'And so humble about his achievements!'

'I wouldn't be surprised,' said the physicist, 'if he gets the Nobel Prize.'

Meanwhile, feeling neglected up on the ceiling, Brittany lifted a glass of water from the table below her head and took a small sip. Or tried to. It's difficult drinking when the glass is pointing up and your head is pointing down.[5]

19 Problems with being de-gravitised: Problem #2 – trees and street signs

'I don't know what you're grumpy about,' said Brittany's

[5] Don't try this at home.

mother, Joanna, as they made their way out into the parking area behind the television studios. 'Most people would give their right arms to be guests on "Famous People".'

'All they did was talk about Dad.'

'That isn't true,' said Joanna. 'And Mr Beam was so nice to you after you choked on your water and turned bright crimson. Did he let you keep that handkerchief?'

'I don't want his silly handkerchief!' Brittany said.

Her mother looked up at her. 'Can I have it if you don't want it, Brit?'

'MUM! WATCH WHERE YOU'RE GOING!'

It was only three days since Brittany's twelve-hour Gravity Buster ride and people still weren't used to dragging her round on the end of a piece of string like a helium-filled balloon.

'Sorry,' said Joanna, tugging her daughter down out of the branches of the tree she had just walked under.

'You're worse than Marie Curie!' Brittany grumbled, spitting out a leaf.

Marie Curie was their Saint Bernard dog. Last night she had taken Brittany out for her evening walk and caught her on a street sign. Brittany had been stuck there for nearly an hour before a man with a ladder came out of a nearby house and untangled her. She had nearly died of embarrassment when she saw who it was – Mr Hoolihan, her teacher.

'Why weren't you at school today?' he'd asked.

20   Birds?

'I got the whole interview on tape,' Lukas said when they arrived home. 'Do you want to watch it?'

'Later.' Pulling off her Doc Martens, Brittany let them fall all the way to the floor. Clump! Bump! Joanna frowned but didn't say anything. She was probably still feeling guilty about the tree.

'Hey, I loved the bit where you drank the water,' Lukas said.

Brittany rolled her eyes. Little brothers! 'Were there any phone calls?'

'Only someone from the newspaper.'

'Are they going to ring back? They were going to do a full-page story on me.'

'They didn't want you, they wanted Dad.'

'Dad?' Brittany nearly tripped on the smoke detector. 'I thought they'd be sick of writing about dumb toads by now!'

'It's not toads they're interested in,' Lukas said. 'It's birds.'

Joanna raised her eyebrows. Brittany lowered hers.

'Birds?' they both said together.

21   Yes, birds!

Here's what had happened. Remember *Bufo lemmingitis*, the virus Mr Hu developed that made cane toads think they were fish? Well, it had an unexpected side effect. Birds were starting to catch it. Right up and down the east coast of Australia, birds of every description were flying to the beach, jumping in the water and then swimming out to sea.

It was a disaster! Nobody minded all the cane toads swimming away, but everyone (except, maybe, the worms) was upset about the birds doing it.

Suddenly Brittany and Lukas's father was no longer famous, he was *infamous!* (Have you looked it up yet?)

22   All Augustus's fault

Mr Hu was late home from work that night. It was nearly eight o'clock when his white CSIRO four-wheel drive pulled into the carport. Lukas helped him carry a big pile of books inside.

'Did you see Brit on "Famous People"?'

Augustus stepped carefully over Marie Curie, fast asleep on the doormat. 'No. It's been a rather hectic day.'

Brittany was lying on her stomach on the kitchen ceiling doing her homework. She looked down when her father came in.

'Hi, Dad.'

'Hi, Brit. How was the interview?'

'Embarrassing. I choked on my drink.'

'That was the best bit!' Lukas dumped his load of books on the table. 'I got it on tape. Do you want to have a look, Dad?'

'Not now, Lukey. I haven't had dinner yet.'

Joanna came in from the study. She gave Augustus a kiss, then picked up one of the books. *Birds of the Southern Ocean.* 'Is it true about the birds, Augustus?'

He nodded. 'I've been down at the beach all afternoon trying to shoo them back to shore.'

'Did you see Mr Rankin's pigeons?' asked Lukas. Their next-door neighbour bred champion racing pigeons. Some of them were worth thousands of dollars.

Augustus turned white. 'Have Mr Rankin's pigeons gone?'

'This afternoon. He was hopping mad!'

'I'd better go next door and apologise.'

Joanna placed a hand on his arm. 'Wait until tomorrow, Gus. Let him cool down a bit.'

'Maybe you're right,' Augustus agreed, sounding relieved. Mr Rankin's other hobby was riding motorbikes. He was part of a gang called the Bone Crunchers. 'The whole thing is a complete disaster!'

Brittany, almost right above them, noticed a tiny brown and white feather in her father's hair. 'What's all the fuss about anyway? Don't birds float?'

'They do,' said her father. 'But they're floating away.'

'How far away?'

'Right over the horizon.'

'What a laugh!' said Lukas.

'It isn't funny.' Augustus sat down at the table and opened one of the books at a chapter about albatrosses. 'I've got to find an antidote,' he said. 'Or soon there won't be a single bird left in Australia. And it'll all be my fault.'

23   What it means to be infamous

Next day a large photo of Augustus appeared on the front page of the newspaper. Below it, in huge type, were two words:

BIRD BRAIN!

24   Aaaaargh!

'Aaaaargh!' Brittany groaned, folding the newspaper and dropping it onto the couch far below her head.

The story about her was only six lines, in very small type, on page twelve. Worse, they had printed the photo of her upside down, which made her look the right way up. No wonder she wasn't famous!

25   Problems with being de-gravitised: Problem #3 - school

'Brittany, get *back* to your desk!'

'I can't, Mr Hoolihan – I'm stuck!'

Sydilly Central Primary School had been built 101 years ago and, like many old buildings, it had very high ceilings. Mr Hoolihan had to place one desk on top of another one, then a chair on top of that, before he could reach Brittany's string. Somehow he managed to climb up and haul her safely back down.

'You'll have to get a longer leash,' he puffed, looking very red in the face.

Brittany spent the rest of the day tied to her chair. Her chair was tied to her desk. But she couldn't concentrate on her lessons. Mr Hoolihan had stacked a mountain of encyclopaedias on her desk to keep it (and her) from shooting up to the ceiling, so all she could see was *McFunk & Wagnalls, McFunk & Wagnalls, McFunk & Wagnalls, McFunk & Wagnalls, McFunk & Wagnalls*. Twenty-six times. To make matters worse, she felt dizzy. You see, sitting right side up is actually upside down to someone who has been de-gravitised. All the blood went to her head (well, not *all* of it, but more than should have been there) and her face turned red and blotchy. Luckily, no one could see it on account of the encyclopaedias. All they could see were her pigtails poking up[6] over the wall of books like the ears of a rabbit that hadn't yet learned how to play hide-and-seek properly.

26 It's lucky birds can fly

That night, Augustus came home early from work. He took his shoes off at the door and tipped the sand out of them into one of Joanna's pot plants.

'I was just down at the beach,' he said.

Joanna looked worried. 'Were there many birds?'

'Thousands!'

'Oh dear.'

Augustus spread his arms and did a little dance, leaving sandy footprints across the carpet. 'It's wonderful, fantastic! They're coming back. The sea makes them better!'

'I don't understand,' Joanna said.

'The lemming virus only lasts 24 hours once the birds start swimming out to sea. There must be something in the sea water that cures them. After 24 hours they stop behaving like fish and' – he began beating his arms up and down like wings – 'they come flap, flap, flapping back to shore!'

'That's marvellous!' laughed Joanna as Augustus took her in his arms and danced her around in a circle.

Marie Curie, who ever since she was a puppy had thought she was human, leapt up against the dancing couple and crashed them into the telephone table.[7]

---

6 Problem #4 – hair.

7 Moral: 120 kilogram Saint Bernards can't foxtrot.

'What's all the racket about?' asked Lukas, poking his head round his bedroom doorway.

Joanna lifted the telephone off the floor. 'The virus – it only lasts 24 hours after the birds go into the sea.'

'So that's why all Mr Rankin's pigeons came back today,' Lukas said.

'Did they? Fa-a-a-a-antastic!' sang Augustus. 'Marie Curie, would you like the next dance?'

Sitting in the curve of the archway that led through to the lounge room, Brittany had a horrible thought. 'What about cane toads?'

Augustus dogtrotted Marie Curie across the hall rug and back. (Over went the telephone again.)[8] 'What *about* cane toads?' he asked airily.

'Do *they* get better after 24 hours?'

'I hadn't thought of that.' He stopped dancing and Marie Curie licked his face. 'It's quite possible, I suppose.'

'Bummer!' said Brittany.

Everyone frowned up at her, puzzled.

'Don't you see?' she said. 'If the toads get better, they might come back too!'

Augustus blew a bit of dog drool off his lip. 'They won't be able to.'

'If they swim *out*, why can't they swim *back*?'

'Ocean currents,' he explained. 'After 24 hours the toads would be right out in the Pacific currents, which would sweep them *away* from the land. It would be like trying to swim uphill.'

Swimming uphill didn't sound so difficult to Brittany, but her mother heaved a big sigh of relief. 'It's lucky birds can fly.'

'Oh my gosh!' Brittany gasped. She had just remembered

---

[8] Moral: They can't actually dogtrot, either.

something. That day on the Gravity Buster, when she had seen all those birds flying past, she had also seen something else – two birds that *weren't* flying.

'Emus,' she whispered. 'Emus *can't* fly.'

Augustus went pale. 'Oops!' he muttered.

27   Oops, indeed!

It was true. All the other birds managed to fly back to shore once the sea had cured them of the virus, but not the emus. The emus were stuck. After 24 hours swimming out to sea they became caught in the strong, offshore currents that Augustus had talked about. When they stopped thinking they were cane toads (which thought they were lemmings, which thought they were fish) and turned round and tried to swim back to shore, the emus found themselves going backwards, being swept further and further away from land.

Something had to be done – and quickly – otherwise soon there wouldn't be a single emu left in Australia!

28   Operation Emu

That Friday another large photo of Augustus appeared on the front page of the newspaper. Below it was printed the following story:

HU LAUNCHES OPERATION EMU

Ingenious CSIRO scientist, Dr Augustus Hu, yesterday announced a bold plan to save our emigrating emus.

Following the accidental infection of Australia's bird population with the cane-toad virus, *Bufo lemmingitis*, large numbers of emus are presently swimming out to sea. It is feared the birds might drown or end up in New Zealand.

Dr Hu has requested the aid of every boat owner in the country to help rescue our emus. At dawn tomorrow, an estimated three million craft will set forth from our shores on Operation Emu, the largest peacetime rescue operation in history. Witnesses from the *McGuinness Book of Records* are flying from Britain to verify the record.

Dr Hu plans to direct the rescue himself from his six-metre yacht, the *Bananana*.

29 Problems with being de-gravitised: Problem #5 - hats

'Of course you have to wear a hat,' said Joanna, as the bright yellow *Bananana* sailed out past the lighthouse early next morning amidst a fleet of boats of every size and shape.

'But it keeps falling off!' Brittany complained.

She was bobbing about at the top of the flagpole, where her father (who actually wasn't a very good sailor) had secured her string in a most unseaworthy granny knot.

35

'Tie it on, then.'

'The cord's strangling me!'

Lukas was looking on with interest. 'What's the use of a hat if she's upside down? It isn't her head that will get sun-burned, it's her feet.'

Joanna considered this. 'You're right.' Clambering back to the flagpole, she hauled her daughter down into the boat. 'Now, let's make you sun smart...'

A couple of minutes later Brittany was wearing *two* hats. One on each foot.

30 Flangle

Here's another new word. You won't find this one in your dictionary because it has only just been invented. Flangle is the opposite of dangle. It's when something dangles *up* instead of *down*. You only use it for things which have been de-gravitised and tied to pieces of string.

31 Emu spotter

'Emu ahoy!' Brittany cried several hours later.

Having her act as the fleet's emu spotter was Lukas's idea. They tied her to a very long rope and paid it out until she was flangling 40 metres above the *Bananana*. From there she was able to spot swimming emus before anyone else.

'Where is it?' yelled a woman in a nearby launch.

Brittany pointed to the distant emu. 'Over there!'

The blue and white launch roared off in that direction.

'Do you want a bite to eat?' Joanna called up to her.

'Yes, please. And a drink.'

Augustus hauled her back down and hitched her to the rail. 'How's it going up there?'

'Hot,' Brittany said, taking a sip from her drink (it was in a plastic bottle with a straw) and watching three black cockatoos swim past. 'What's in the sandwiches, Mum?'

'Ham and jam.'

'I'll have jam.'

'Not ham *or* jam,' Joanna said, 'ham *and* jam. Your brother made the sandwiches.'

'Good one, Lukas!'

Lukas wasn't listening. He was watching the blue and white launch chug past towing an emu behind it on the end of a short rope. 'I wish *we* could rescue one.'

Brittany did too. But she said nothing. The important thing was that the emus were being rescued. Already the boats around them had towed 35 back to shore. And the same thing was happening right around the Australian coast.

'Could I have another sandwich, please?' asked Brittany.

'Careful,' Lukas warned her. 'You'll get seasick.'

'I never get seasick,' she said smugly.

32 Problems with being de-gravitised: Problem #6 - airsickness

Picture this. It's 25 minutes later. Lukas is sitting in the stern of the *Bananana*, fingers trailing in the water, day-dreaming about what he's going to do in the school holidays

(trap one of the wild pigeons in
the City Mall and ask Mr Rankin
to help him train it). Suddenly he
hears what sounds like a seriously
out-of-tune kookaburra directly
above him. He looks up.

Big mistake.

33   Trouble with birds

Brittany had been having trouble with birds.[9]

Not emus, thank goodness, but other birds. Smaller ones.
Birds that had recently recovered from their 24-hour doses
of *Bufo lemmingitis* and were flying back to shore.

They thought she was a tree and kept landing on her.

It was an understandable mistake. Put yourself in the
birds' position. There you are, fifteen or twenty kilometres
offshore, you're tired and hungry, probably feeling a bit
confused about things (I mean, if you're a desert parrot,
for example, you probably hadn't even *seen* the sea until
yesterday), when suddenly, right there in front of you,
40 metres up, is this upside-down person with two straw
hats on its feet. What would your first reaction be?

'Ho hum, an upside-down flangling human.'

Not likely.

'A tree!' you'd probably think. 'Excellent! I think I'll take
a breather.'

The ones that landed on Brittany's hats weren't too bad.
But the ones that settled on her arms, her clothes, her chin,
were a pain. One particular kind of honeyeater kept sticking
their beaks into her ears. Swallows seemed to want to build

[9] Problem #7 – birds.

nests in her hair. A northern rosella (with very long claws) landed on her back and clung there where Brittany couldn't reach it for nearly fifteen minutes.

The very worst ones of all were two wedge-tailed eagles. It probably would have been okay if there was only one, or if they had visited separately, but when both of them landed together, one on each hat, their combined weight was more than Brittany's anti-weight.

Do-
o-
o
o
o
O
O
W
N

everyone went.

Splash! into the sea.

Both eagles promptly let go and flapped wetly away, leaving Brittany, suddenly weighing less than nothing again, to shoot back up to 40 metres like someone doing an upwards bungy jump. *Sproing-g-g-g-g!* When she hit the top of the rope's extension she nearly lifted the *Bananana* right out of the water.

34   Eric

It was almost dark when Lukas finally got his wish (*one* of his wishes – the other one had to do with putting on dry clothes).[10]

---

[10] After what happened in Chapter 32, Lukas had to jump into the sea fully clothed.

'Emu ahoy!' Brittany shouted.

Augustus looked round. The *Bananana* was the last boat left. All the others had disappeared back towards land towing emus behind them.

'Looks like this one is ours,' he said, busily shaking nutmeg onto the main brace.

'It's *splice*,' Joanna told him, 'not *spice*.'[11]

They dragged Brittany down from the sky and secured her to the flagpole. Then they sailed over to the emu. It was bobbing about in the waves like a giant, raggedy swan. Augustus steered the yacht slowly past it while Lukas leaned out and dropped a lasso neatly over its head.

'Can we keep it?' he asked.

'No,' said Joanna.

'Please!'

'Absolutely not,' said Augustus. 'It's a wild animal.'

'Bird,' Brittany corrected him.

'It doesn't look wild,' observed Lukas. He settled himself in the stern holding the emu's rope. 'Eric,' he said, smiling at his new pet. 'Eric the emu.'

35   Chooks

Halfway back to shore they passed two bantam hens swimming flat out in the other direction. Frowning beneath his captain's hat, Augustus peered after them.

'Didn't they look like Ginger and Meggs!'

[11] This is seafaring talk. If you don't understand it, ask a pirate.

Joanna leaned over the side and scooped a small brown egg out of the waves. 'Whose turn was it to lock up the chooks last night?'

'Brit's,' said Lukas.

'Lukas's,' said Brittany.

Augustus brought the *Bananana* slowly around and set out after Ginger and Meggs.

36   The show's over (not!)

The sun had set by the time the *Bananana* made it back to shore. But the city was lit up as it always was on Saturday evenings, so a lot of people saw the strange procession making its way up from the pier.

First there was Lukas, with Eric on his lead. Then there was Joanna, with Brittany on hers. And last came Augustus, herding Ginger and Meggs along in front of him.

Someone took a photo of them as they cut across the car park outside a busy McNoodles restaurant. The sudden flash from the camera sent Eric into a panic and he took off. Well, he didn't actually take off (he was an emu, after all) but he *dashed* off, dragging poor Lukas out onto the street, straight in front of a bus!

Luckily the bus wasn't moving – it was parked there with nobody in it. But the incident gave everybody a big fright.

'No more photos, please!' Augustus said to the crowd, taking Eric's lead from Lukas and putting him in charge of Ginger and Meggs. 'The show's over.'

He was wrong. Nobody knew it at the time, but the show had only just begun.

37   Erica

They locked Eric up with Ginger and Meggs for the night. Augustus planned to release him next day. But when Joanna went out in the morning to see if the bantams had supplied them with any eggs for breakfast, she got more than she bargained for.

'Hey, guys,' she called in through the back door. 'Come and look at this!'

At first glance it looked as if someone had been playing lawn bowls in the chook pen. Bunched up in the far corner like strange, misshapen bowling balls were eight huge dark-green eggs.

'Awesome!' said Lukas. 'Eric's a mum.'

'Eric-*a*'s a mum,' Joanna corrected him.

'Now we'll *have* to keep him...I mean her,' said Brittany, who had come outside as far as the end of the pergola, where she was standing upside down in her floppy dressing-gown like a huge fruit bat.[12]

'Not necessarily,' said Augustus.

They all looked at him.

Rubbing his hands vigorously together, he gave an evil grin. 'Let's have a really big omelette!'

---

[12] Joanna had sewed elastic stirrups to the bottom of Brittany's dressing-gown to stop it flopping down over her head. In fact, lots of Brittany's clothes had to be altered, and she couldn't wear skirts and dresses at all. It was a real problem; in fact it was: Problem #8 – clothes.

'D-a-a-a-a-a-a-d!' said Brittany and Lukas.

'Augustus!' said Joanna.

'Woof woof!' said Marie Curie (who really liked omelettes).

Augustus sighed. 'I suppose we can keep her until the babies have hatched.'

'That's *if* they hatch,' said Joanna. She pointed. 'Erica doesn't seem particularly interested in them.'

It was true. The emu was down the other end of the chook pen, nibbling at the wire to see if it was good to eat.[13] Lukas walked round outside the enclosure. He looked up at her and shook his finger.

'Erica, go and sit on your eggs!'

'She's probably hungry,' said Brittany.

Joanna frowned. 'What do emus eat?'

Augustus frowned too. 'More to the point – how *much* do they eat?'

38   Two answers

(i)   fruit, leaves, insects

(ii) a lot

39   Operation Emu, part 2 (and 3, and 4, and 5, and...)

'Heave ho, me hearties!' Augustus said as soon as everyone had finished breakfast (cereal, toast, fruit, leaves, insects, a bone). 'It's time to weigh anchor.'

'Huh?' said the crew.

'Set sail,' explained Captain Hu, grabbing his sailor's hat.

[13] It wasn't. See Chapter 38.

'Operation Emu, remember?'

'That was yesterday.'

'Yesterday, today, tomorrow. We'll have to keep doing it until all the emus have been rescued.'

'But we *did* rescue them all, Dad!'

'We rescued all of *yesterday*'s lot. There'll be more swimming out today. And more tomorrow. And more the next day. Operation Emu won't be over until every emu in Australia has made it to the ocean and been rescued. It might take weeks.'

'It might take forever,' sighed Lukas.

They all looked at him.

'Think about it,' he said. 'One day all the rescued mother emus are going to lay eggs, and when the eggs hatch the babies will catch the virus and then there'll be *more* emus to rescue. And when the female babies grow up, *they'll* lay eggs, and...'

'Yes, we get the picture,' said Joanne.

'Oops!' said Augustus.

40   Chooks

'What about chooks?' asked Brittany.

'What *about* chooks?' her father asked.

41   Operation Chook

Next day Augustus's photo was in the newspaper *again*.

EGG ON FACE

Infamous CSIRO scientist, Dr Augustus Hu, was further embarrassed yesterday when it was revealed that his cane-toad virus, *Bufo lemmingitis*, posed a serious threat to Australia's poultry industry.

"Chooks are very poor flyers," he explained. "So, like emus, once they catch the virus and swim out to sea, they'll have to be rescued."

Mrs Sharon Greenaway, president of the newly formed Sea Range Eggs Association, yesterday joined with Dr Hu in launching Operation Chook 'N' Emu, the largest peacetime rescue operation in history.

Representatives from the *McGuinness Book of Records*, returning to Great Britain after witnessing the first phase of Operation Emu on Saturday, last night changed planes in Singapore in order to come back and witness the event.

42 Not fair

'It isn't fair!' Brittany grumbled.

Joanna was doing the crossword in a *Whoever* magazine. 'What isn't fair, darling?'

'Dad's in the newspapers all the time.'

'I'm sure he doesn't want to be.'

'That's what's so unfair,' Brittany said. '*He* didn't go on the Gravity Buster a million times! *He* didn't become degravitised! *He* doesn't have to flangle all day on the end of a rope! The soles of *his* feet don't get sunburned!'
(Problem #9 – sunburned feet.)

'You should wear your hats.'

Brittany picked at a fly-spot beside her on the ceiling. 'Eagles keep landing on them. Plus, there was that currawong last week that thought the hats were nests and tried to eat my toes.' (Problem #10 – currawongs.)

'I know it's difficult for you, dear,' Joanna said, looking up from her crossword. 'But I'm sure that as soon as this bird crisis is over, Dad will work out a way to make you normal again.'

'I don't *want* to be normal – if I was normal I wouldn't be famous!'

'Then what are you complaining about?'

'When I go on TV I want them to talk about me, not about how super-wonderful Dad is. I want to be on the front page of the newspaper instead of page twelve. I want people to ask for my autograph!'

Joanna climbed up onto her chair and offered Brittany her pen and magazine. 'Please would you give me your autograph?'

Brittany giggled. Taking the pen, she flipped the *Whoever* open in the middle...to a huge colour photograph of her father!

43 Meggs to the rescue

Here's an interesting fact about emus – the mothers lay the eggs, the fathers sit on the nests.

This created a bit of a problem in the Hus' chook pen. Since Erica wasn't Eric, she had no inclination to sit on her eight eggs after she'd laid them. That was Eric's job. But where was Eric? *Who* was Eric? He might have been any one of the thousands of rescued emus roaming the streets of Sydilly. He might even have been still swimming out to sea, somewhere far over the horizon, next stop New Zealand!

Luckily, Meggs the bantam came to the rescue. Meggs had always wanted to have chicks but every time she laid an egg, one of the humans found it and took it away. So when she noticed a whole nest of orphan eggs in one corner of the pen, and when she realised nobody else seemed interested in them, the game little bantam climbed up on top of them (which was quite a feat: they were the most humungous eggs she had ever laid eyes – much less bottom – on) and took over the job of being their mum (or should that be dad?).

44 Street-birds

Operation Chook 'N' Emu had been running for nearly six weeks and everyone was growing thoroughly tired of it. Each morning a huge fleet of boats would sail out to sea. Each afternoon they would return in ones and twos towing emus behind them, their decks loaded down with chooks.

And each evening a whole new lot of birds would catch the disease and swim out to sea.

Some poultry farmers tried caging their birds in, but it was discovered that once they had *Bufo lemmingitis*, the chooks stopped eating and wouldn't lay eggs until they were cured. The only way to cure them was to allow them to swim out to sea.

Emus were the same. But emu farmers had an extra problem to deal with – broken fences. Once an emu caught the disease, *nothing* was going to stop it getting to the sea. After a while, emu farmers began leaving their gates open at the first sign of the disease in their flocks, rather than have their fences wrecked.

There was another problem too: returning the birds to their proper homes after they had been rescued. Poultry farmers began putting address tags on their birds' legs and offering a small reward for their return. Emu farmers did the same. Soon a fleet of trucks, utes, panel vans, billycarts, cars with trailers, cars without trailers (but with sun roofs for emus to stick their heads through), retired drovers, even schoolkids with supermarket trolleys, waited at the piers every afternoon for the boats to come in and then transported the rescued birds back to the farms, hatcheries, zoos, parks, pens and backyards they had come from.

This worked okay for the domestic birds. But the wild emus were different. Most of them came from far inland, and the difficulty of transporting them all the way to Oondooroo, for example, or the Gibson Desert, or even the Back of Bourke, was too much. Besides, no one was going to get paid for doing it. So the boat owners who rescued them simply let the wild emus go as soon as they reached the shore.

As a result, there was soon a huge population of homeless emus living in and around Australia's coastal towns and cities. These 'street-birds' became a huge problem.

Emus weren't exactly suited to city life. They didn't know the road rules and caused humungous traffic jams. They barged into shops and ate the money out of the tills.[14] They knocked over china displays and trampled furniture. They helped themselves at fruit stalls; they chased skateboard riders and poodles and women with big hats;

[14] Amendment to Chapter 38: (i) fruit, leaves, insects *and* money.

they disrupted wedding receptions (they particularly liked those little sugar brides and grooms on the tops of the tall white cakes)[15]; they terrorised diners at outdoor cafes and messed up people's gardens.

The last straw occurred when three particularly street-wise emus invaded Parliament House and chased all the Cabinet ministers into the back benches.

'This has gone quite far enough!' gasped the Prime Minister, who, squashed up next to the Leader of the Opposition against the back wall, certainly could not go any further. 'Something has to be done about the street-bird problem.'

45   But what?

'I've got no idea,' said Augustus.

He was talking to three men in pinstriped suits who had come knocking on the Hus' front door late one Thursday evening.

'Well, think of something!' said the largest and most heavily pinstriped of the three.

Augustus scratched his head. 'I've been racking my brains but I haven't been able to come up with anything.'

Pinstripe Number One pulled a long buff-coloured envelope from inside his jacket. 'Here's a letter from the Prime Minister directing you to devote all your energies to solving the street-bird problem.'

Brittany, curled up on the ceiling with a book, tried to read the letter over her father's shoulder but she was too far away. All she could see was the Prime Minister's big signature at the bottom.

[15] Amendment to Chapter 38: (i) fruit, leaves, insects, money *and* sugar brides and grooms.

'Dad, can I have the autograph?'

All four men looked up at her.

'Good heavens!' said Number One. 'How did you get up there?'

'It's a long story,' said Augustus. 'But if you're really interested, there's a book about it called *The Upside-down Girl*.'

'I haven't got time to read books,' Number One said dismissively. He turned back to Brittany's father. 'What should I tell the Prime Minister?'

'Tell him I'm looking into the problem.'

'Looking into it!' spluttered Number One. 'Mr Hu, this is a national crisis! The Olympics are only a few months away. How will it look to our international visitors if our cities are full of street-birds? We'll be a laughing stock! You absolutely *must* do something about them.'

'I am already doing something,' Augustus pointed out. 'Every day I go out in my boat to direct the rescue operation.'

'Well, you can stop doing that for a start. The Prime Minister wants you back in your laboratory working on a cure.'

'Then who's going to look after Operation Chook 'N' Emu?'

Number One spent a moment straightening his pin-stripes. 'The P.M. is taking care of it.'

46   The Navy to the rescue

Next morning the entire Australian Navy swung into action. Every frigate, destroyer, corvette, submarine, dinghy, patrol boat and rubber duck in the fleet joined the task of rescuing *Bufo lemmingitis*-affected chooks and emus from the sea.

Spotter planes, huge Air Force Orions, and *chup-chup-*

chupping helicopters darted back and forth across the sky like busy dragonflies.

Way out in space, a Top Secret ASIO satellite silently altered its Top Secret orbit and began using its Top Secret surveillance cameras to pinpoint the position of chooks and emus that had drifted out of Australian waters. These were then rescued by Bottom Secret submarines.

Instead of releasing the rescued emus on the beach like everyone else did, the Navy flew them far inland by helicopter and released them in their natural habitat hundreds of kilometres from the coastal towns and cities.

At lunchtime, Augustus stood outside his laboratory watching a Navy helicopter fly overhead in roughly the direction of Uluru. Dangling below it, with their several heads and two-times-several legs poking out of a large teardrop-shaped net, were several newly rescued emus.

'If only...' Augustus muttered, then trudged back inside to his books and microscopes and test tubes.

47   If only what?

'...emus could fly,' Augustus said at dinner that night.

Brittany, sitting on an upside-down canvas chair that Joanna had attached to the ceiling with macrame and cup-hooks, nearly choked on a right-side-up forkload of spaghetti. (Problem #11 – eating spaghetti.)

'*What* did you say, Dad?' she asked, fishing a strand of spaghetti out of her right nostril.

'I said, "If only emus could fly."'

48   Hu the cat dragged in

'Look what the cat dragged in!' said Ben.

'I'm not a cat,' Lukas pointed out, dragging Brittany by her leash across the platform towards the Gravity Buster.

'And I'm not a what,' Brittany said haughtily. 'I'm a Hu.'

Ben grinned up at her flangling just above her brother's head. 'As if I could ever forget our most famous passenger!'

Brittany blinked happily. Famous! 'Can you do us a favour, Ben?'

'Not if it's what I think it is.'

He pointed to a large sign on the wall.

1 RIDE LIMIT
no PERSON IS ALLOWED MORE THAN **1** RIDE
On THE GRAVITY BUSTER

'We call it the Brittany Rule,' he said. 'The management came up with it in your honour.'

Brittany was pleased – not many people had rules named after them. Also, it meant that nobody else could become de-gravitised like she was. But she did feel a bit guilty. 'Don't worry,' she said, 'we don't want a ride.'

Ben frowned. 'What *do* you want?'

'Hold my sister for a sec,' Lukas said, passing him Brittany's leash. Then he slipped off his bulging backpack very carefully, as if it contained something fragile (eggs, for instance). 'We want you to de-gravitise something for us.'

49 Ernest, Evangeline, Engelbert, Elizabeth, Edward, Elly, Estha and Eggy

One week later, Lukas went out to feed the chooks (and emu) after dinner. And came running back inside.

'They've hatched! Erica's eggs have hatched!'

Everyone raced out to the chook pen to have a look. Everyone, that is, except Brittany, who couldn't go further than the end of the pergola without llafing up into space.

'What are they like?' she called, but nobody seemed to hear her. Her parents and Lukas and Marie Curie were all in the chook pen, crowded round Meggs and her newly hatched brood. Never had a bantam hen looked prouder than Meggs did of the eight gangly chicks that towered over her.

'Hull-o-o-o-o!' Brittany said. 'Can anybody hear me?'

Mr Rankin's shaved head popped up over the fence. He was holding a pretty, greeny-blue pigeon in his enormous hairy hands. 'What's all the racket about?'

'Good evening, Seymour,' Augustus said from the chook pen. 'Our emu eggs have hatched.'

Mr Rankin didn't return the greeting, nor did he offer congratulations. 'I hope this isn't another of your experiments, Augustus.'

Lukas straightened up. He was holding one of the chicks. 'We're simply helping out, Mr Rankin. You see, the eggs' mother wouldn't sit on them.'

Their next-door neighbour nodded his bristly head. 'Just make sure they don't re-infect my pigeons,' he said gruffly, then disappeared back behind his fence.

Brittany called over to Lukas, 'Can I hold one?'

He brought Evangeline over to her. (Actually, it might not have been Evangeline – have you ever tried telling baby emus apart?) The chick was fat and fluffy and covered in black, brown and white stripes.

'Don't get too attached to it,' Augustus warned, noticing the way Brittany was cuddling Evangeline (or Ernest, or Engelbert, or Elizabeth, or Edward, or Elly, or Estha, or Eggy). 'Now that the eggs have hatched, we'll have to release them.'

'Dad, *no*! We can't let them go!'

Her parents exchanged glances. Joanna said, 'Brittany, we've talked about this before. Erica belongs in the wild and so do her young.'

Brittany kissed the emu chick's funny little feet. (She was upside down, remember, and Baby E was the right way up.) 'A dingo might get them, or a wild cat, or they might fall in a hole and get stuck!'

Then she remembered something. Lifting baby Evangeline (or Ernest... etc.) down level with her face, she took a close look at her (or his) sides. Yes, there were stubby little wings!

Almost as if the chick knew what Brittany was thinking, it began wobbling them up and down.

'Look!' said Joanna, smiling. 'It doesn't know it's an emu – it's trying to fly!'

Brittany held the baby bird out at arm's length. And let it go.

'Brittany, what are you...!' began her father. Then his mouth fell open.

Everyone (well, nearly everyone) watched in amazement as the chick flew across the yard, back in through the open door of the chook pen, and bowled poor Meggs over in a cloud of sawdust, feathers and flying straw.

50   Flying emus

'So you see,' explained Lukas, 'we got Ben to strap my back-pack, with the eggs inside it, under one of the seats of the Gravity Buster.'

'And then,' Brittany cut in, 'we left it there for six hours.'

'Which is exactly half how long Brittany went on it.'

'So the chicks are *half* de-gravitised!'

'They weigh *half* what a normal emu chick weighs.'

'And even though their wings are tiny...'

'They're big enough to fly with!'

Augustus was still shaking his head like someone who had just seen a UFO. He bent and carefully picked up Elly. That's just a guess, actually, because Elly looked exactly like Edward, who bore an uncanny resemblance to Estha, who was a dead ringer for Ernest, identical brother of Eggy and Elizabeth, mirror images of each other and of Evangeline, who even Meggs couldn't tell apart from Engelbert, who looked so much like the others that nobody was sure which one he was (even Engelbert wasn't sure – he thought he was either Elly or Edward). Anyway, Augustus picked up whoever it was and tested its weight in the palm of his hand.

'You're right. It's as light as a feather!'

At this, Baby E flapped its stubby wings and shot three metres straight up into the air.

Lukas and Brittany gave each other the thumbs up. (Actually, Brittany's was a thumbs down.)

'Dad, you've got your wish,' said Brittany.

'We've invented flying emus!' said Lukas.

51 Operation Up, Up and Away!

For the next four and a half weeks the Gravity Buster was closed to the public. Its only passengers were emus. They were herded on in lots of twelve, strapped in and given six hours of free rides. As soon as they were released, they pranced round for a bit, running in circles and jumping high into the air as they slowly got used to weighing almost nothing. After a while they discovered that if they stuck their little feather-duster wings out when they were at the top of a jump, they could glide softly back down to earth instead of falling in an untidy heap. Then, after about fifteen more minutes of bouncing and jumping and gliding, they usually worked out how to flap their wings.

Remember what happened to Baby E? Well, it was the same with adult emus. Here's how Augustus recorded it in his workbook:

1 semi-degravitised emu + flapping wings = up, up and away!

He was right. Soon they were no more than a bunch of small, long-legged dots in the sky.

52   Flight instructor

Throughout Operation Up, Up and Away, Augustus spent at least twelve hours a day at Loony Park fussing over the emus that were about to go on the Gravity Buster and looking after those that got off. He even acted as a flight instructor for the ones that didn't get the hang of flapping their wings straight away.

When the first twelve de-gravitised emus flew off into the sunset, five separate television crews filmed Augustus waving goodbye.

Brittany nearly died of embarrassment when they all watched the news that night. There was her father, on national TV, making a complete idiot of himself!

'Oh Dad!' she groaned, watching him running round in circles flapping his arms like wings. 'Famous people aren't supposed to act like that.'

Lukas flicked a rubberband at her up on the ceiling. 'You're just jealous because Dad is always on TV and you aren't.'

'I'm not!' Brittany's face went bright red. 'I'd rather not be on TV than have everyone laughing at me.'

Augustus, who didn't seem to care what people thought of him, pointed at the screen. 'That's something I hadn't realised. Look, I'm not raising my right arm quite as high as my left one.'

'Who cares about your arms?' cried Brittany. 'You look like a galah!'

Augustus did some practise arm-flaps there on the couch. ('Ouch!' said Joanna.) 'I would have thought,' he puffed, 'that galahs had a longer downstroke.'

'Perhaps you had better not flap inside, dear.'

'Pardon?' he muttered.

'Don't flap!' Joanna said, rubbing her shoulder.

Augustus didn't seem to hear her. It didn't matter anyway, because he had already stopped flapping. He seemed to be in a trance. His eyes were glued to the screen where a flock of emus flew bumpily up into the sky.

'Have you ever in your whole life seen such a beautiful sight?' he asked dreamily.

53   Word quiz

Do you know what *notorious* means?

If you don't, now would be a really good time to look it up in the dictionary.

54   What goes up, must come down

Four and a half weeks later, Augustus was in the newspaper yet again.

FLYING EMUS FLOP

Following a directive from the Prime Minister yesterday, notorious[16] CSIRO scientist, Dr Augustus Hu, will stop creating flying emus.

"The operation has not been a success," Dr Hu admitted. "From tomorrow I shall be returning to my laboratory to search for another solution to the street-bird problem."

Operation Up, Up and Away was to have rid Australia's cities of emus. It was hoped that once they could fly, the street-birds would return to their outback homes. This has not proven to be the case.

[16] I told you!

"Unfortunately, emus don't seem to have any sense of direction," Dr Hu told our reporter. "They don't know where they come from, therefore they cannot go back there."

Since the advent of Operation Up, Up and Away, many of the homeless emus that formerly crowded our cities' streets are now crowding our cities' skies. This has created a whole new set of hazards, not only to aircraft, construction workers and TV antennas, but to bare-headed pedestrians, babies in prams, weather forecasters and volleyball players.

With the Olympics only months away, the Prime Minister has directed Dr Hu to work day and night on the problem.

"If Sydilly isn't cleared of street-birds by the Opening Ceremony," the Prime Minister said yesterday, "we'll be disgraced before the eyes of the whole world!"

55   They can't shoot them!

'Why can't they just catch them and return them to the outback like the Navy are doing?' Brittany asked as she and her father drove to work next morning.

It was the school holidays and Brittany was helping out at the laboratory. She was earning $5 an hour for cleaning the ceilings and light fittings.

'It's nearly impossible to catch a flying emu,' Augustus said.

'But most of them *can't* fly.'

Augustus slowed the car as a gang of street-birds shot across the intersection ahead of them – straight through a red light. 'I know. But the ones on the ground are even *harder* to catch! You would have to clear the entire city of traffic and then go in with nets.'

'Sounds like fun,' said Brittany, who was holding one of the chicks on (actually, under) her knee.

'To stop a city for a day would cost millions of dollars,' Augustus pointed out.

'So what's going to happen? The Prime Minister said they've got to be gone by the Olympics.'

'If I can't come up with a solution by then,' – Augustus stared straight ahead through the windscreen – 'they're going to send in the Army.'

'What will the Army do?'

'Shoot them.'

'No!' Brittany hugged Elizabeth (or whichever one it was) to her. 'They can't shoot them!'

'They can,' her father said grimly. 'They will.'

'Then you've *got* to think of something, Dad!'

'I'm doing my best,' he said quietly.

56   Square two

'Eureka!' Augustus cried two hours later.

They were in the laboratory where he was doing experiments on a blood sample he had taken from Elizabeth.

'What is it, Dad?' Brittany's voice came from somewhere overhead.

'Remember how Mr Rankin was worried that Erica's babies might re-infect his pigeons? Well, it can't happen.'

'Of course it can't!' Brittany scoffed. 'His pigeons have already had it!'

'Another reason it can't happen,' her father said, 'is that the babies can't catch *lemmingitis* in the first place.'

'Why not?'

'Erica seems to have passed on her immunity to them.' Augustus was bent over a big electronic microscope which contained a smear of Elizabeth's blood on a glass slide. 'It appears that if an adult bird has had the disease, its chicks won't catch it.'

Brittany's and Elizabeth's heads popped down out of one of the skylights. 'Excellent! Then Ernest, Evangeline, Engelbert, Elizabeth, Elly, Estha and Eggy won't swim out to sea!'

'You left out Edward.'

'Him too. Dad, that's fantastic! It means no more birds will get sick. You're a genius! The problem's over!'

'If I was a genius none of this would have happened in the first place.' Augustus straightened up. 'And the problem is far from over. Our cities are still full of homeless emus.'

'Bummer,' said Brittany, remembering what the Army would do if her father didn't come up with a solution in time. She picked up Elizabeth, who she'd been using as a feather duster, and hugged her. 'Back to square one.'

Augustus took his binoculars over to the window. 'Not exactly square one,' he muttered, watching a flock of very large, long-legged birds circling high overhead.

57 Llafing off the world

Here's something you have probably been wondering about. What would happen if Brittany's string snapped? Or if she went sleepwalking one night and stepped out of a window? Or if she fell off the end of the pergola? In other words, what happens to a de-gravitised person if they llaf off the world?

Let's find out...

'Yiiiiiiiiiiiiiiiiiiiiiiiiiiiiiiiieeeeeeeeeeeeeeeeeeeeeeeeeeeeeeeeeeeeeeeeeeeeeeeeeek!'[17]

58 How it happened (a really long chapter)

I had better tell you how it happened.

Remember how the Hus' Saint Bernard dog, Marie Curie, used to take Brittany for walks? Well, on this particular day (a Sunday), Ernest, Evangeline, Engelbert, Elizabeth, Edward, Elly, Estha and Eggy wanted to come along too. They were ten weeks old now and becoming quite large. With all eight of them living in the chook house, plus Erica, who took up a lot of room, and Meggs and Ginger, who *seemed* to take up a lot of room because they were always rushing about fussing over the Baby Es, it was becoming very crowded. Everyone needed to get out and stretch their legs (and wings).

[17] The yell someone makes when they llaf up into the sky.

'Okay,' Brittany said, clipping her long walking-leash securely to Marie Curie's collar before she flangled out the back door in the direction of the chook pen. 'We'll *all* go.'

So that's what happened – they all went. Even Meggs and Ginger. Erica tagged along at the rear keeping a sharp eye out for ladies in hats, skateboard riders and other interesting things to chase.

This unusual little procession made its way to a nearby park, where Ernest, Evangeline, Engelbert, Elizabeth, Edward, Elly, Estha and Eggy became involved in a boisterous game of hide and squeak. Meggs and Ginger were soon fossicking about amongst the gardens for berries, snails and other tidbits, while Erica went off on her own searching for cyclists. Brittany clipped her leash to a park bench so Marie Curie could go for a romp.

An elderly couple, strolling past with umbrellas, stopped when they noticed her flangling above the wrought-iron seat.

'Are you all right, dear?' asked the old woman.

'I'm fine, thank you.'

'You appear to be upside down,' observed the old man.

'I've been de-gravitised.'

'Aaah!' they both said, nodding gravely.

The man asked: 'Is it painful?'

'Only if the soles of my feet get sunburned.'[18]

'Does it make you dizzy?' enquired the woman.

'Only when I get caught in whirlwinds.' (Problem #12 – whirlwinds.)

The man peered out from beneath his umbrella, then ducked quickly back under it as Eggy (or Engelbert) went sailing overhead, closely pursued by Ernest (or Elly). 'Lot of emus about today. You ought to be careful, young lady.'

[18] Refer back to Problem#5 – hats.

'I'm not worried about emus,' Brittany said. She decided not to say they were hers because the old couple didn't seem to be emu-lovers.

The man used his umbrella to point across the park. 'Is that your dog?'

Brittany gave a little pou[19]. 'Her name's Marie Curie.'

'That's an unusual name,' said the old woman.

'She was a famous scientist. She won the Nobel Prize.'

'What a clever dog!'

Brittany giggled. 'The *first* Marie Curie won the Nobel Prize. My one has never won anything.'

'You ought to give her a prize,' said the man. 'Look, she's bailed up one of those beastly birds.'

Brittany turned and looked. Oh no! One of the Baby Es was hopelessly tangled in the topmost branches of a huge monkey-puzzle tree.

'Please, can you take me over there?' she asked.

The woman seemed puzzled. 'Why do you want to go over there?'

'To rescue it.'

'Rescue it?' spluttered the man. 'You must be out of your mind, young lady!'

Brittany was becoming frantic. 'It's stuck! We've got to help it. Please take me over there!'

'I've a good mind to call the emu catcher,' the man grumbled.

[19] An upside-down nod.

The emu catcher would take it away to the Emu Pound. It would never see its brothers and sisters or its mother (or Meggs, who it thought was its mother) again.

'Please, please, please,' Brittany begged. 'It's only a baby!'

The old couple looked at each other.

'It's just a baby, Herbert.'

'But it's a baby *emu*, Shirley.'

Shirley gazed up into the tree. 'It looks frightened.'

'I'll call the emu catcher,' muttered Herbert.

'Oh, don't be such a meanie!' said Shirley.

'All right, all right,' he said. 'No need to get your bloomers in a knot.'

Herbert unclipped Brittany from the park bench and took her, flangling above his head like a second umbrella, across to the monkey-puzzle tree. The little emu – it looked like Evangeline or Ernest (but actually it was Edward) – was tangled in the very top branches. Brittany's leash was too short to allow her to reach it.

'I'll have to climb up.'

'Be careful, young lady,' said Herbert, guiding her over to a large branch and, once she had a firm grip, releasing the lead.

'Don't fall!' called Shirley.

'She won't fall,' Herbert said with a chuckle, 'she'll fly!'

He meant it as a joke, but – as everyone was soon to find out – he was right.

With the leash dangling down past her head, Brittany began slowly making her way feet first up through the branches. She was upside down, so the climbing part was quite easy – it was like climbing down, not up. But the hanging-on part was murder!

You're probably wondering how the monkey-puzzle tree got its name. Well, it's because it's the only tree in the world that a monkey can't climb. 'Why?' you ask. Because instead of being covered with bark like a normal tree, every millimetre of a monkey-puzzle tree is covered with sharp little spikes. Another good name for it would be the barbed-wire tree. That's how bad they are to climb.

Brittany didn't know it at the time (she does now), but she was making history as she painfully made her way up through the monkey-puzzle tree's prickly branches. She could have gone in the *McGuinness Book of Records* as the first person ever to climb one. It's a record that would have lasted forever.

Slowly Brittany inched her way up through the spiky branches – 'Ouch! Ouch! Ouch! Ouch! Ouch! Ouch! Ouch! Ouch! Ouch!' – while on the ground Marie Curie and Meggs and Ginger and Herbert and Shirley and Erica looked up with worried faces; and not on the ground Ernest, Engelbert, Elizabeth, Edward (I was wrong about it being Edward stuck in the branches – it was Evangeline), Elly, Estha and Eggy flew circles and loops and big, zigzaggy spirals around the tree.

At last Brittany got to Evangeline (or was it...Elly?) and began untangling her. The poor emu was trussed up like an Egyptian mummy, only they wrapped mummies in strips of cloth, not barbed wire. It took ages to undo the tangled chick.

'There you go,' Brittany breathed, gently unwinding the final prickly branch from Elly's raggedy, mussed-up feathers. 'You're free!'

And she tossed him[20] out into the sky.

Unfortunately, Eggy had lost every single one of the feathers from his left wing during his short, painful entanglement in the monkey-puzzle tree, so he could no longer fly. Correction: he *could* fly, but only in very tight circles. So when Brittany tossed him out into the sky beyond the monkey-puzzle tree's topmost branches, Eggy whizzed back round like a deflating balloon and hit Brittany – *poomfff!* – square in the face.

'Ouch!' Brittany cried. And lost her balance. And llef.

'Yiiiiiiiiiiiiiiiiiiiiiiiiiiiiiiiieeeeeeeeeeeeeeeeeeeeeeeeeeeeeeeee
eeeeeeeeeeeeeeeeeeeek!'

59   What goes up, must...go up!

Shirley and Herbert and Meggs and Ginger and Marie Curie stood at the foot of the tree gazing up into the sky. (Erica had galloped off after a passing cyclist.)

'Oh, my!' said Shirley.

'I hope she isn't afraid of heights,' said Herbert.

'Grrrrrrrrrrr!' said Marie Curie.

'What's the matter with the scientist?' Shirley asked.

'It isn't a scientist, it's a dog.'

'Imagine that – a dog winning the Nobel Prize!'

'I don't think that's what happened,' said Herbert. He shaded his eyes. 'Should we do something about the girl?'

'We could call the fire brigade.'

'Their ladders wouldn't be long enough.'

'The police, then. They could send a helicopter.'

'How high do helicopters go?'

'Not *that* high,' Shirley said, peering up at the two tiny (and getting tinier) dots in the sky.

[20] It was actually Eggy.

'Yiiiiiiiiiiiiiiiiiiiiiiiiiiiiiiieeeeeeeeeeeeeeeeeeeeeeeeeeeeeeeee
eeeeeeeeeeeeeeeeeeeeeek!'

60   Can you figure it out?

Did you notice something funny about that second-last
sentence? You're right, it said 'two'. Two tiny dots. Not *one*
tiny dot, which is what you would expect to see if you looked
up at a de-gravitised person busily llafing off the world, but
two of them. Two tiny dots. Can you figure it out?[21]

61   A noisy chapter

'Yiiiiiiiiiiiiiiiiiiiiiiiiiiiiiiiiieeeeeeeeeeeeeeeeeeeeeeeeeeeeeeeeee
eeeeeeeeeeeeeeeeeek!'
   (Are you getting sick of hearing that? Sorry. But, you
see, llafing off the world is pretty scary.)
   'Yiiiiiiiiiiiiiiiiiiiiiiiiiiiiiiiiiieeeeeeeeeeeeeeeeeeeeeeeeeeeeee
eeeeeeeeeeeeeeeeeeeeeek!' yiiiiiiiiiiiiiiiiiiiiiiiiiiiiiiiiieeeeeeeeeeeeeeeee
eeeeeeeeeeeeeeeeeeeeeeeeeeeeeeeeeeeeked Brittany as she
shot up into the sky.
   For several weeks she had been worrying about something like this happening. She had even asked her father
about it. 'If I llef off the world, Dad, how high would I go?'
   'I'm not sure,' Augustus had answered. 'You might just
keep going.'
   'You mean, like, for*ever*?'
   'Well, maybe not forever, but almost certainly you'd go
too high.'
   'Too high for what?'
   Her father had looked uncomfortable. 'To breathe,' he
said finally.

[21] For an answer to this and other questions (for example: Will Brittany
ever stop *screaming*?) go to Chapter 63.

'To breathe?' Brittany echoed.

Augustus nodded grimly. 'You see, the higher you go, the less oxygen there is.'

He had meant she would die.

'I'm going to die!' Brittany thought now as she shot up out of the monkey-puzzle tree and feeted[22] flat out for outer space. No wonder she did all that yiiiiiiiiiiiiiiiiiiiiiiiii-ieeeeeeeee eeeeeeeeeeeeeeeeeeeeeeeeeeeeeeeeking!

62   Sorry, there is no Chapter 62

63   Eggy to the rescue

After llafing flat out for about 1500 metres, Brittany felt a gradual change of speed. Something seemed to be tugging at her, slowing her down. She stopped screaming (phew!) and looked up – which was actually down. Three metres below her was Eggy. Like Brittany, the little emu was also upside down, but unlike her he was flapping like mad.

It took Brittany only about two seconds to work out what had happened. When Eggy had accidentally knocked her out of the tree, the loop at the end of her leash had lassoed him around one leg as it went zipping past. So when Brittany llafed up into the sky, she dragged the little emu behind her. Eggy, naturally enough, didn't want to take a trip into outer space. He was upside down and all he could see was the park and the city and the world getting smaller and smaller. He started flapping desperately to get back down to earth.

It was a losing battle. Eggy weighed only 1400 grams, whereas Brittany, on the other end of the leash, weighed

---

[22] Feeted – the opposite of headed.

minus 37 kilograms. Also, there was the little emu's damaged wing to take into consideration. No matter how fast and hard he flapped, he was still being dragged upwards.

'Go, Eggy!' Brittany encouraged him. 'Fly! You can do it!'

But she knew he couldn't. He had managed to slow them down a bit, but they were still llafing upwards at an alarming speed. The park looked tiny now, as did Sydilly. In fact, it would have been a very nice view to someone who wasn't upside down and feeting flat out towards Mars.

'We're *both* going to die!' Brittany thought.

But there wasn't any need for Eggy to die with her, she realised. He wasn't 100% de-gravitised like she was. If he wasn't connected to her, he would be free to glide safely back down to the ground. With trembly fingers, Brittany fumbled to undo the knot where her leash was tied around her middle.

64   Meanwhile, back in the park...

Herbert and Shirley and Meggs and Ginger and Marie Curie were still staring up into the wide blue sky.

Shirley was counting. 'Five...six...seven...eight.' She stopped.

'Is that it?' asked Herbert.

'That's it. Eight.'

Herbert shook his head. 'Well, I can only see one.'

'That's the girl. She's bigger than the others.'

'It doesn't look like a girl.'

'You need your eyes tested, Herbert.'

'There's nothing wrong with my eyes.
It's these glasses.'

'They're your reading glasses,' Shirley told him.

Herbert took them off and examined them. 'Well, blow me down!' he said, then put them back on. 'So, how many did you say there were?'

'Eight,' said Shirley. 'Nine, if you count the girl.'

'And they're right above us?'

'Directly overhead.'

Herbert opened his umbrella. 'We'd better take cover, then.'

65 He ain't yvaeh, he's our brother

Brittany couldn't undo her leash. The knot was too tight.

'I'm sorry, Eggy!' she sobbed.

Upside down at the other end of the leash, the little emu was still desperately flapping his wings, gamely trying to drag both of them back down to earth. But it was no good – Brittany was too big and yvaeh[23]. Poor Eggy started to tire. His little wings began slowing down. And the slower they went, the faster both he and Brittany shot up into the sky.

They were really high now. Brittany could hardly make out the park. It was just a small green square, about the size of a tissue, among the patchwork of orange roofs, miniature backyards and busy, crisscrossing streets. The whole of Sydilly looked no bigger than a map. In fact, it looked exactly *like* a map, except bits of it were moving. Miniscule cars beetled to and fro along skinny streets. A toy emu chased a toy cyclist across a parking lot. Seven little brown dots came flapping up out of the park…

Huh? *Seven little brown dots?*

Brittany blinked her eyes to make sure she wasn't imagining things. No, they were real – it was Ernest,

[23] Yvaeh, pronounced eevay, is the de-gravitised form of heavy. If you weigh minus 37 kilos, for example, you aren't heavy, you're yvaeh.

Evangeline, Engelbert, Elizabeth, Edward, Elly and Estha, and they were coming to the rescue!

'Eggy,' Brittany gasped with relief, 'we're saved!'

And for a while it did look as though they were going to be saved. When Eggy saw his sisters and brothers flying up from below, he seemed to find his second wind. Suddenly he was flapping harder than ever, and he and Brittany slowed right down. Ernest, Evangeline, Engelbert, Elizabeth, Edward, Elly and Estha began gaining on them. Soon they were only 200 hundred metres below. Then the distance was 150 metres... 110 metres... 100 metres... 90 metres... Their would-be rescuers got to within 50 metres before Eggy began to tire again. His flapping slowed. The distance remained at 50 metres for a while, then his sisters and brothers began to fall back slowly – 55 metres... 60 metres... 85 metres...

'Eggeeeeeeeeeeeeeee!' Brittany cried in desperation as she and Eggy hurtled up into space. 'Please, please, please try to flap harder!'

But it was no good. Eggy was pooped. And with every passing second, Ernest, Evangeline, Engelbert, Elizabeth, Edward, Elly and Estha were falling further and further behind.

66   Meanwhile, back home...

Augustus was out on the front lawn holding out a handful of breadcrumbs.

'Coo, coo, coo, coo[24]!' he was calling softly.

Two of Mr Rankin's pigeons were perched on the roof.

'Coo, coo, coo, coo!' Augustus cooed.

In his other hand, hidden furtively behind his back, he clutched the smooth wooden handle of Lukas's yabby net.

---

[24] 'Coo, coo, coo, coo' in pigeon-speak means 'Come and have a bite to eat, my little lovely!'

'Coo, coo, coo, coo!'

The pigeons looked down at him in an interested kind of way, but they didn't move.

After three or four more minutes of this, Augustus let out a small, frustrated sigh and stomped into the garage. He emerged 30 seconds later with a long aluminium ladder, which he leaned against the guttering on the front of the house. Clutching the net in his left hand, he climbed gingerly onto the roof. The pigeons watched curiously as he scooped the breadcrumbs out of his shirt pocket and held them out on the palm of his proffered right hand.

'Coo, coo, coo, coo!'

Neither bird moved. They were less than four metres from him, perched on the ridge at the top of the roof. Crawling on his knees, Augustus inched his way up the steeply sloping tiles.

'Coo, coo, coo, coo!' he cooed, closing the distance with every second.

When he was two metres away, the nearer pigeon stood up and fluffed its feathers as if it was about to take flight. Augustus froze. Behind his back, the fingers of his left hand sweated on the handle of the net. He still wasn't quite close enough. 'Easy does it,' he thought. He slid his right knee forward five centimetres, then his left. Both birds seemed alert now, their heads cocked suspiciously sideways. One false move, Augustus knew, and they'd be gone. Slowly he extended his right hand and began sprinkling the bread-crumbs on the tiles in front of him. 'Coo, coo, coo, coo!'

The closer pigeon fluffed its feathers again, then it leaned forward and took two small hops towards the crumbs.

'Yessss!' Augustus thought, his heart beating very fast as

his left arm tensed to swing the net up, over and down on the unsuspecting bird. 'Just a few more hops,' he thought, 'and you're mine!'

That was when it happened. A huge shadow fell across him and both pigeons shot away towards Mr Rankin's house in a frantic whirring of wings.

Clunk! Clunk! A pair of black, horny feet landed on the tiles a metre from Augustus, then a long snake-like neck ending in a massive triangular beak flashed into view. *Ratta-tat-tat-tatt!* it went against the tiles, and all the breadcrumbs were gone.[25]

Still on his knees, Augustus looked up angrily at the wild emu that had ruined his pigeon-hunt.

'Hoy!' he cried.

One of the worst things you can say to an emu is 'hoy'. You see, in emu-speak, 'hoy' means: 'I say, you do look rather like a wombat's bottom!'

In the blink of an eye (Augustus's left one) the insulted bird whipped its head up, round and pecked him – *thunk!* – right in the middle of the forehead.

Taken completely by surprise (and, anyway, it hurt!), Augustus took a wobbly knee-step backwards, lost his balance and fell. He rolled all the way down the roof, crashed over the guttering and landed heavily on the steps below.

'Owwwwwwww!' he wailed, which in emu-speak means: 'I love you, you gorgeous feathery hunk!' and caused his assailant, who happened to be a female, to peer over the edge of the roof and flutter her long eyelashes at him.

Augustus, however, felt anything but lovey-dovey towards the emu. You see, in human-speak, 'Owwwwwwww!' can mean a lot of things, and one of them is: 'Oh bother, I think I've broken my leg!'

---

[25] Amendment to Chapter 38: (i) fruit, leaves, insects, money, sugar brides and grooms *and* breadcrumbs.

67   Owwwwwwww!

At the same time as her father was learning to talk like an emu, Brittany was flying like one. Here is how it happened.

Shortly after we left her and Eggy, at the end of Chapter 65, llafing helplessly into the wide blue yonder with Ernest, Evangeline, Engelbert, Elizabeth, Edward, Elly and Estha in hot pursuit, Brittany had a brainwave. She remembered seeing her father on television teaching newly semi-degravitised emus to fly. He had been flapping his arms like wings.

'I can do that!' she suddenly thought.

Nearly 3000 metres above the earth, upside down and out of control, feeting straight up and dragging Eggy behind her, Brittany started madly flapping her arms.

It worked! She and Eggy began slowing down. The seven little emus following them began catching up again. But very, very slowly.

'Eggy,' Brittany puffed. 'You'll have to help me!'

Eggy, of course, didn't understand what Brittany was saying, but he *did* notice that his sisters and brothers were gaining on them and that gave him his second (third, actually) wind. Summoning up all his remaining strength, he began flapping as fast and as hard as he could. Between the two of them, the upside-down emu and the upside-down girl nearly stopped their upwards llaf.

Thirty seconds later, Ernest (or was it Elizabeth?) caught up with them and grabbed Brittany's leash in his (or her) beak. Then the others arrived. All seven of them positioned themselves along the leash, turned upside down, and began flapping back down to earth.

It took nearly half an hour. But finally the strange little procession of eight upside-down emus and one upside-down girl arrived back at the park, where Shirley grabbed the leash and tied it firmly to Marie Curie's collar.

'My word!' said Herbert. 'You certainly gave us a scare, young lady.'

Brittany, puffing with exhaustion after all that flapping, rubbed her aching arm muscles. 'I gave *myself* a scare!'

'Never mind, you're safe now,' he said. And gave her arm a big, reassuring squeeze.

'Owwwwwwww!'

Eight tired little emus fluttered their eyelashes at her.

68   Ceilinged

When Joanna learned what had happened, she gave Brittany an enormous hug. Which was kind of awkward because Brittany's nose ended up squashed against her mother's belt, and one of her knees bumped Joanna square in the jaw. (Problem #13 – hugging.)

'If it wasn't for Erica's chicks,' Joanna said, blinking away sudden tears, 'we might have lost you!'

Brittany gave a big gurhs[26]. 'Lucky they were there.'

'Lucky they could fly,' said Lukas.

'Lucky *I* could fly!'

'You mightn't always be so lucky,' Joanna warned.

Brittany hit the roof (her mother had just let her go). 'I promise I'll be more careful next time.'

'There won't be a next time. From now on, young lady, you're not to set foot out-of-doors unless an adult is with you.'

'Or Marie Curie?' Brittany put in hopefully.

'Marie Curie's a dog.'

'But she's an *adult* dog!'

Joanna shook her head. 'I'm serious about this, Brittany. You're to stay inside.'

[26] An upside-down shrug.

'That's not fair! You can't ground me if I haven't *done* anything.'

'You're not grounded...' her mother began.

'You're ceilinged!' Lukas cut in.

Joanna tried hard not to smile. 'For your own good, Brittany, I want you to stay indoors. Just until this anti-gravity thing has worn off,' she added.

'It's not going to wear off, Mum. I'll be like this forever.'

'At least you'll stay famous,' said Lukas.

'I'm not famous!' Brittany stamped her foot on the ceiling and made all the light fittings rattle. '*Dad*'s the one who's always in the newspaper!'

69   Not again!

'Fraid so. Next day there was *another* big picture (this time of Augustus on a stretcher) and *another* front page story.

HU SAYS HOY

Hopes of ridding Sydilly of emus before the Olympics took a tumble yesterday when CSIRO scientist, Dr Augustus Hu, fell from the roof of his house and broke his leg in four places.

Hu, the man allegedly responsible for the emu invasion, admitted the accident was his own fault.

"I should never have said 'hoy' without first checking my emu dictionary," he said.

The scientist had been working on an antidote for the cane-toad virus, *Bufo lemmingitis*, when the fall occurred.

A spokesnurse from Sydilly Hospital, where Hu was resting uncomfortably last night, reported his condition as fractious.

'HOW DARE
THEY CALL ME
FRACTIOUS!' Augustus
roared, flinging the
newspaper across the
ward. 'I'LL SUE THEM!'

Brittany imagined the headline: **HU TO SUE!**

'Please don't,' she said. This morning's headline had been
bad enough. All day at school people had been tugging her
leash and saying, 'Hoy!'

Joanna was drawing a smiling face on Augustus's
enormous plaster cast. 'They were referring to your leg, Gus,
not your mental state.'

'Then they should have said fractured.'

'It isn't fractured,' Brittany said. 'It's broken.'

Augustus grinned up at her. 'I stand corrected.'

'You *lay* corrected,' corrected Lukas.

'It's *lie*, not *lay*,' his father corrected him back. 'Don't
they teach you anything at school?'

'Lots of stuff.' Lukas waited until Joanna had finished writing a soppy message under the smiling face, then started a message of his own. 'Today we learned what notorious means.'

'So what does it mean?'

'You.'

'Me!!!?' spluttered Augustus.

Lukas, pen in hand, was bent over his father's plaster cast, biting the tip of his tongue in concentration. 'We're doing a class project on flying emus and we had to look up all these words from the newspaper articles. What does "hoy" mean?'

'Never you mind.'

'I said it to Engelbert and he pecked my knee.'

'You're lucky he wasn't taller.'

'They're growing really fast,' said Brittany. She was standing directly above Augustus's bed, right between two slowly twirling ceiling fans. 'And I've noticed something else – they're getting heavier.'

Her father nodded absent-mindedly. 'You grow, you put on weight.'

'But they're putting on *heaps* of weight. They can hardly fly any more.'

'That's not what I heard. Yesterday they flew pretty high, by all accounts.'

'I know.' Brittany frowned. 'But it was really hard for them. It was much easier flying down than it was up – which is kind of weird because on the way down they had to drag me behind them.'

'Maybe *you're* putting on weight,' Lukas suggested.

Brittany didn't say anything. Well, she *did* say something but it had nothing to do with Lukas's smart comment...

71 Problems with being de-gravitised: Problem #14 - ceiling fans

'Ouch!'

72 Don't get smart, smartypants

'I've been thinking,' Lukas said in the car going home.

'That makes a nice change,' Brittany murmured, rubbing her sore leg.[27]

'It's something for you, so don't get smart, smartypants.'

'You're the one who said I was getting fat, fathead.'

'I didn't say anything about getting fat. I was talking about putting on weight.'

'It's the same thing.'

Lukas shook his head. 'No it isn't. Fat is about shape, weight is about gravity.'

The car went over a bump and Brittany flangled to the full extent of her seat belt. 'So how do I put on gravity?'

'Well, Dad's plaster cast gave me this excellent idea...'

73 Papnssiw?

At the exact same moment that Lukas was talking about their father's plaster cast, Augustus, propped up in his hospital bed, was reading what everyone had written on it. There were three messages.

One said: Love you, Smushkins
Another said: **Lukas 4 ever!**
The last one went: *pap n ssiw*

27 See Chapter 71.

'Papnssiw?' Augustus said aloud, a deep frown creasing his forehead. 'Whatever does that mean?'

74 Plan A

Lukas had mixed up a load of wet concrete in Augustus's wheelbarrow.

'And now we pour it into the gumboots...'

'Hang on a minute!' Brittany protested. She was standing on her hands on the underside of a plastic crate that Lukas had wedged into the low ceiling of the garden shed. Her feet and a good part of both her legs were enveloped in a pair of Size 14 gumboots which Lukas had positioned on the floor directly below her. 'How am I supposed to get out once the concrete has set?'

Lukas scratched his head. 'I hadn't thought of that. Do you need to get out?'

'Of course I do! You don't expect me to spend the rest of my life cemented into Dad's gumboots?'

'You look quite good in them, actually. Black's definitely your colour.'

'Very funny!' Brittany pulled her feet out of the enormous rubber boots and collapsed up onto the crate. 'It was a good idea, Lukas, but I'd rather be stuck on the ceiling than stuck in concrete, thank you very much.'

Lukas gave the wheelbarrow's gooey grey contents a stir with the shovel. 'It seems a shame to waste this stuff.'

'We don't have to waste it,' Brittany said, noticing a pair of buckets hanging from the ceiling beside her. 'There's always Plan B.'

75 Plan B (or: How to wreck a perfectly good pair of Doc Martens in one easy lesson)

Take two twelve-litre plastic buckets and drill two ten-millimetre holes in the bottom of each. Push four large coach bolts down through the holes so that the threads poke out the bottom. Next, fill both buckets nearly to the top with slushy concrete. While the concrete is still wet, press a Size 1 Doc Marten boot into each bucket, making sure that the laces stay clear of the surface and that *no concrete goes inside the boots.* Leave for 24 hours to dry.

Now find two skateboards. (There's probably an old one out in the shed and you can get the other one at a garage sale for about $5.) Using the bolts poking out of the buckets as a guide, drill two ten-millimetre holes through the tops of both skateboards. Push the bolts through the holes and attach nuts to the underside. Do the nuts up really tight and, hey presto, you're the proud owner of a pair of twenty-kilogram Doc Martens on wheels![28]

76 Push

'I can't move!' said Brittany.
'Here,' Lukas offered, 'I'll give you a push.'

> *Dear Reader,*
> *The rest of Chapter 76 seems to have gone missing.*
> *The publisher apologises for this incovenience and hopes the remainder of the book will make some sense without it.*

[28] Otherwise known as roller-buckets.

77   Paper noses in winter

'What's *papnssiw*?' Augustus asked the patient in the other bed.

'You tell me.'

'No, *you* tell *me*! You wrote it, after all.'

'Wrote what?'

'*Papnssiw.*'

'How could I write "papnssiw"? I don't even know how to spell it.'

'I-T.'

'Very funny! I was talking about "papnssiw".'

'P-A-P-N-S-S-I-W.'

'Sounds like some sort of secret code.'

Augustus nodded. 'I've spent two whole days trying to work it out. And most of the nights as well,' he added, yawning. 'At first I thought it was an anagram – that all I had to do was put the letters in a different order and it would make sense – but the best I could come up with was "snip paws", "pip swans" and "swap pins".'

None of those made a whole lot of sense, the other patient agreed. 'Maybe some of the letters are missing.'

'I've tried that, too,' said Augustus, who loved a good puzzle better than almost anyone. 'Paper noses in winter. Pa pinches silver wallet.' He heaved a sigh of defeat. 'Are you absolutely certain you didn't write it?'

'One hundred percent.'

Augustus shook his head. 'I was sure it was you. Otherwise you must have written either Love you, Smushkins or **Lukas 4 ever**, and that doesn't make any more sense than *papnssiw* – I mean, if Mum and Lukas wrote them they do make sense, but not you. That only leaves *papnssiw*, so I kind of figured you and it went together.'

'What *are* you talking about?'

'This!' Augustus pointed to the third of the three messages written on his plaster cast: *pap n ssiw*. 'It's driving me crazy! I've got to know what it means!'

'Miss you dad,' said the other patient.

'Miss me? How can you miss me, we're practically on top of each other!'

'It's what it says.'

'Huh? It says *papnssiw*, clear as day.'

'From here,' the other patient said, 'I see *miss u dad, miss u dad, miss u dad*.'

Augustus peered closely at the cast. Then he tipped his head to one side. 'Oh, I se-e-e-e-e-e-e-e!' he said slowly, and laughed. 'Upside down! I hadn't thought of that.'

'It's what I think about all the time,' Brittany said from her bed on the ceiling. A single tear fell from her right eye and landed – *splat!* – right on the first *S* of *Smushkins*. 'I'm so sick of being the wrong way up!'

'Never mind, sweetheart,' said mushkins[29]. 'It won't last forever.'

Brittany felt annoyed. Everyone was telling her that lately. 'Of course it will!'

'You're wrong, you know.' Augustus lay back on his pillows and looked straight up at her. 'I've had a lot of time to think over these last couple of days. And while I mightn't have solved the great "papnssiw" mystery, I did figure out how de-gravitisation works.'

'So how *does* it work?'

'Do you want the good news or the bad news?'

Brittany didn't hesitate. 'The good news.'

'You'll get your gravity back.'

84   [29] The ink wasn't waterproof.

If she didn't have six hands, Brittany would have attempted to clap them. She settled on wriggling her toes (all 30 of them) instead. 'And what's the bad news?' she asked nervously.

'It'll take seven years.'

78   Everything you wanted to know about re-gravitisation but didn't know who to ask

'It was what you said about Erica's chicks gaining weight that put me onto it,' Augustus explained. 'You see, Ernest, Evangeline, Engelbert, Elizabeth, Edward, Elly, Estha and Eggy are growing really fast. And growing involves the production of new body cells. Now, these new cells weren't around when Ernest and Co. went on the Gravity Buster, so the new ones are perfectly normal.'

'You mean they've got gravity?' said Brittany.

'Exactly. And as more and more new cells are produced, they are slowly outnumbering the old, de-gravitised ones. So it's no wonder the baby emus are finding it harder and harder to fly.'

'Wait a minute!' said Brittany. 'I'm growing too – why aren't I gaining weight?'

'You are.' Augustus tried to read the chart dangling from the foot of the bed bolted to the ceiling almost directly above his own. *Patient's weight: minus 32 kilos.* 'But much more slowly than Erica's chicks. You see, you were a lot bigger to start with – more than half grown – and remember you've been fully de-gravitised, whereas Ernest and Co. were only half de-gravitised.'

'So how do you figure I'll be normal again in seven years? If I'm *more* than half grown now, when I'm fully grown *less* than half of me will be made up of normal, heavy cells.'

'Ah,' said Augustus, and raised one hand dramatically. 'Here you have to take into account the body's continual renewal process. You see, our body cells are constantly dying and being replaced by new ones. Over a period of seven years, this happens to every single cell in your body.'

'So in seven years I won't be me?'

'You'll be you, all right, but you'll be made up of a totally new set of cells – and all of them will be normal, gravitised ones.'

Brittany tried to adjust her pillow, a tricky job for someone with six hands. 'Seven years is a long time.'

'It won't ee oh aab.' The rest of Augustus's words were muffled by Brittany's pillow, which had landed square on his face. He removed it and tossed it back up to her. (She caught it with her teeth.) 'It won't be so bad,' he continued. 'There'll be little milestones along the way. In about three years time, for example, you'll weigh exactly nothing.'

'I own aa oo air o-ee oss ahinz!' Brittany said. (Which, when spoken by someone without a pillow in their mouth, might have sounded like: 'I won't have to wear concrete Doc Martens!')

The rest of Chapter 76

Dear Reader,
The publisher is delighted to inform you
that the rest of Chapter 76 has turned up. Here it is . . .

'Yiiiiiiiiiiiiiiiiiiiiiiiiiiiiiiiiiiiiiiiiiiiiiiiiieeeeeeeeeeeeeeeeeeeeee
eeeeeeeeeeeek!'[30]

76a   A bonus (and very loud) chapter

CRASH![31]

---

[30] The cry someone makes when pushed down a skateboard ramp
wearing twenty-kilogram roller-buckets.
[31] The sound of someone wearing twenty-kilogram roller-buckets
colliding with a pigeon house.

79   Pigeons

'What about the fence?' Augustus asked.

'Straight through it,' said Brittany.

'You should see the hole!' said Lukas.

It was the following day. Lukas had come to visit them in hospital. He and Brittany were describing Brittany's accident to Augustus.

'But it was the pigeon house that stopped me,' Brittany said. 'Otherwise I'd have ended up in Mr Rankin's pool.'

'And that would have been *bad*!' said Lukas.

Their father raised his eyebrows. 'I would have thought seeing three of everything was bad.'

'Not as bad as drowning,' Brittany pointed out. 'I had about 40 kilos of concrete strapped to my feet, remember.'

Her father stared out the window at a flock of emus flying circles around the trees in the hospital gardens. 'What happened to the pigeons?'

'Mum said that because we busted up his pigeon house, Mr Rankin could use our shed to keep them in.'

'Mr Rankin's pigeons are in *our* shed?' Augustus asked. Lukas nodded.

A cunning look crossed Augustus's face. 'Lukey,' he said, motioning his son closer. 'I want you to do me a favour...'

80   Mad scientist

'GET IT OUT OF HERE!' roared the hospital superintendent.

'It's quite tame,' Augustus said. 'It won't hurt anybody.'

'THAT ISN'T THE POINT! THIS IS A HOSPITAL, NOT A ZOO. ABSOLUTELY NO ANIMALS ARE ALLOWED HERE!'

'Actually, it's a bird.' Augustus lifted the pigeon up level with his face. 'Coo, coo, coo!' he cooed. 'Who's a pretty boy, then?'

'They're girls, Dad,' a voice said from directly above them. 'All three of them are girls.'

Startled, the superintendent looked up and noticed Brittany for the first time. His expression changed from angry to puzzled. 'Who are you?' he asked in an almost normal voice.

'I'm his daughter.'

'What are you doing up there?'

'I've got concussion. I see three of everything. They're keeping me here under observation.'

The superintendent still seemed puzzled. 'But why are you on the ceiling?'

'I've been de-gravitised. If they put me in a normal bed, I llaf straight out of it.'

'Haven't I seen you somewhere before?'

'Yessss!' thought Brittany. 'At last someone's recognised me!' She was about to say, 'I was on "Famous People",' when she noticed he was looking at Augustus, not her.

'It's vaguely possible,' Augustus said modestly.

The superintendent's expression began to change. Slowly, a huge smile spread across his face. 'I KNOW WHO YOU ARE NOW!' he bellowed excitedly. 'YOU'RE THAT MAD SCIENTIST WHO TAUGHT THE EMUS TO FLY!'

'Please don't shout,' Augustus said. 'You're scaring Pidge.'

81   No comment, Pidge

Next day a large photo of the Hospital Superintendent appeared on the front page of the newspaper. He was holding a pigeon up towards the camera and grinning like a Cheshire Rat[32].

---

[32] For more about Cheshire Rats, read *Alice's Adventures in Downunderland*, by Brittany Hu.

IS PIDGE RIDGIE-DIDGE?

In an effort to overcome the street-bird problem which is threatening the forthcoming Olympics, Sydilly Hospital will convert one of its wards into a research laboratory, it was announced last night.

Hospitalised after a fall last Sunday, key figure in the crisis, Dr Augustus Hu, will now be able to continue his experiments in his hospital bed. Hu's daughter, injured in a freak skateboarding accident, will assist him.

Hospital Superintendent, Mr Tom Cheshire (pictured here with Pidge the pigeon) hinted that a breakthrough was near.

"Dr Hu believes that Pidge might provide the answer to the homeless emu problem," he said.

When asked what that answer might be, Pidge made no comment.

82 Say cooo!

Augustus, his bed covered in laboratory equipment, poked a tongue-depressor into Pidge's open beak. 'Say aaaah!'

Pidge didn't say anything.

'Say aaaah!'

Pidge still didn't say anything. (Though she did cock her head on one side at the sound of a noisy motorcycle outside.)

'I am vorning you, Ms Pigeon,' Augustus said in a funny voice. 'Ve haff vays off making you talk!'

'They can't,' Brittany said.

'Can't what?'

'They can't talk, Dad – they're pigeons.'

Augustus regarded Pidge thoughtfully. 'Say cooo!'

Before Pidge could say cooo (or even booo, for that matter), the door swung noisily open and Mr Rankin, wearing his black motorcycle helmet, came storming into the ward.

'Where is it?' he demanded, pulling a newspaper out of his leather jacket and pointing at the pigeon photo on the front page.

Augustus had quickly hidden Pidge under the bedsheet. 'Where is what, Seymour?'

Mr Rankin began prowling the ward, opening drawers and looking under beds. 'You know perfectly well what I...'

'Cooo!' Pidge said under the sheet.

Mr Rankin spun round. 'What was that?'

'Choo!' went Brittany. 'Excuse me, I think I'm getting hay fever.'

Mr Rankin looked suspiciously up at Brittany, then suspiciously down at Augustus. There was a large tattoo of a skull on his arm – it looked suspicious too.

'Cooo!' Pidge repeated.

'Bless you!' said Augustus.

Brittany blew her nose.

'As soon as I get home,' Mr Rankin said menacingly, 'I'm counting my pigeons. If a single one of them is missing, I'm going to come back here and tear this place apart!'

Still wearing his helmet, he stomped crossly out of the ward.

'What are we going to do, Dad?' Brittany whispered as soon as their unwelcome visitor had gone. 'Mr Rankin will come back!'

'No he won't,' said Augustus. Lifting Pidge out from under the sheet, he tossed her up into the air. She circled the ward twice, then flapped out through the open window.

Brittany watched the three pigeons flying away. 'Won't they get lost?'

'She's a homing pigeon – homing pigeons never get lost.'

'But how will they find their way home?'

'That's what I'm trying to find out,' Augustus said.

Brittany stared out the three windows where the three Pidges had disappeared. 'I guess you won't find out now.'

Augustus smiled mysteriously and lay back in bed. 'We'll see,' he said.

83   A matter of National Security

Late that night three important-looking men in pinstriped suits paid a visit to Mr Rankin.

'Here's a letter from the Prime Minister,' said the largest and most heavily pinstriped of the three, pulling a long buff-coloured envelope from inside his jacket. 'He wants you to cooperate fully with Dr Hu. It's a matter of National Security.'

Mr Rankin, wearing pyjamas covered in little teddy bears riding motorbikes, slowly read the letter. 'Will I be a kind of secret agent?' he asked.

Pinstripe Number One hesitated. 'Yes, I suppose you could say that.'

Mr Rankin looked behind him to make sure no one else was within earshot, then leaned forward and whispered into Number One's ear. 'So what's my first assignment?'

'Your first assignment,' whispered Number One, 'is to return Pidge to Dr Hu at the hospital.'

84 Cooo-oo coo coo!

'Her name isn't actually Pidge,' Mr Rankin whispered softly so as not to wake Brittany, who was fast asleep in her upside-down bed directly above them. 'It's Iris.'

Augustus yawned. It was one o'clock in the morning. He had been expecting Mr Rankin, but not quite this early. 'Nice to see you again, Iris.'

'Cooo-oo coo coo[33]!' said Iris.

85 Iris boomerangitis

Exactly one week later, Iris made newspaper headlines. There was a nice photo of her on the front page, with Augustus in the background smiling from his hospital bed. (The top of Brittany's head was just visible, badly out of focus, above him.)

[33] Which in pigeon-speak means: 'Nice to see you too, Doc, but please don't go shoving any more of those dirty great sticks into my beak and asking me to speak human!'

IRIS HAS VIRUS

Vainglorious[34] CSIRO scientist, Dr Augustus Hu, yesterday made a discovery that he believes could bring an end to the street-bird crisis.

Working in his hospital ward-cum-laboratory, he has discovered how homing pigeons are able to find their way home from distant places.

"It's caused by a virus that all pigeons contract during infancy," he said.

The virus magnetises the pigeons' brains, making them ultra-sensitive to the earth's magnetic field.

"In effect, their brains become little compasses," Hu explained. "They can find their way home from anywhere in the world."

Dr Hu has named the virus *Iris boomerangitis*, after Iris the pigeon (pictured), with whom he has been working closely during his research.

"All I have to do now is develop a strain of the virus that can be caught by emus," Hu told our reporter. "Then the street-birds will all be able to find their way back to wherever they came from."

86   Delivery for Dr Hu

The Hospital Superintendent's eyebrows would have shot all the way up into his hair except he was bald.

'THIS IS A HOSPITAL, NOT A ZOO!' he bellowed at the small boy leading eight young emus and a red bantam hen in through the hospital's main entrance.

'They're for Dr Hu,' said Lukas.

Mr Cheshire beamed like a you-know-what. 'That's all right then,' he said in a much quieter and altogether more

[34] You'll probably have to look that up, too.

friendly voice. 'Follow me, young man. We can use the Staff Only lift, if you like – it's much quicker.'

87   Down and about

Next day Joanna brought in Brittany's twenty-kilogram Doc Martens. Brittany was up and about (well, down and about) by this time but was finding upside-down life in the hospital quite hazardous on account of all the ceiling fans. (She could see three times as many of them as anyone else and had to wear a pair of Lukas's cricket pads on her legs because she couldn't tell which were the real fans and which weren't.)

'It'll be much better having you down here where things won't fall so far if you drop them,'[35] said Augustus, nodding approvingly as Mr Rankin and two burly male nurses laced Brittany into her Size 1 concrete-filled roller-buckets.

Largely on account of her seeing three of everything, there had been several accidents involving falling glassware during Brittany's first few days as a research assistant. On one occasion, her bedpan had nearly knocked her father unconscious right in the middle of an experiment involving Iris, a magnet, a map of Australia and a piece of cheese.[36] Luckily the bedpan had been empty at the time.[37]

Securely laced in and ready to roll, Brittany found it difficult getting around at first.

---

[35] Problem #15 – dropping things.

[36] 'I can't understand it!' Augustus said when that particular experiment failed. 'It's always worked with mice!'

[37] Problems #16 and #17 – number ones and number twos.

Even attached to skateboards, concrete buckets aren't the most manoeuvrable footwear (and if you're wearing six of them, look out!). So Lukas made a harness out of several old macrame pot-plant hangers from home, and they hitched up Ernest, Evangeline, Engelbert, Elizabeth, Edward, Elly, Estha and Eggy ahead of her like a team of reindeer pulling a sled. (Fortunately Erica's chicks were now too big and heavy to fly – emus and ceiling fans definitely don't mix!) After a few collisions with hospital furniture and one with three nurses, Brittany soon learned to whizz round the ward at speeds that were frightening to watch.

'Careful!' warned Augustus, looking up from his microscope where he was examining a brand new virus called *Emu boomerangitis*. 'Or you'll end up in hospital!'

It took him several moments to realise why Brittany was laughing.

88   Not a people virus

Being upside up after so long upside down was difficult to get used to at first. Everything looked wrong. Up looked down and down looked up. And then there was the dizziness caused by Brittany's de-gravitised blood, all of which wanted to flow up into her head. After a while, everything seemed to be spinning.

'Try not to wobble!' said Augustus, who was about to inject Engelbert (or was it Edward?) with the new virus.

That was easy for him to say, Brittany thought crossly. He wasn't on roller-buckets; his head wasn't spinning; he couldn't see three of everything.

'Could you come a little closer,' he said.

Brittany rolled right up alongside his bed. She was holding Engelbert (or Edward) in her arms. 'I hate needles!' she said, closing her eyes.

'It isn't for you,' – Augustus leaned over with the syringe – 'it's for Ernest.'

'Engelbert,' Brittany corrected him.

The little emu in her arms suddenly struggled (it was Edward, who didn't like being called Engelbert), causing Brittany to open her eyes. The first thing she saw was a glistening needle with a teardrop of yellowish liquid wobbling from its tip. *And it was about to be jabbed into her middle hand!* Actually there appeared to be three needles, but the one on the left, which seemed about to prick her middle hand, was the only one Brittany focused on. Without thinking, she flinched sideways, jerking the middle hand away from the left needle. Which brought her right hand directly into the path of the middle needle.

Something stung her.

'Ouch!' Brittany shrieked, plucking all three hands away, shooting backwards on her roller-buckets and knocking over a tray of instruments.

Edward leapt out of her arms and darted across the ward to join Meggs and his sisters and brothers, who all fussed about him as though *he* was the one who had just been jabbed with a hypodermic needle.

'Oops!' said Augustus.

Brittany clutched her stinging hand. Slowly it dawned on her what had happened. 'Will I die?'

'I shouldn't think so,' her father said, which didn't sound altogether reassuring to Brittany. He examined her hand, then wiped it with a sterile swab. 'It's only a scratch.'

'But the virus! Won't I get the virus?'

Augustus showed her the syringe. It was still full of pale yellow liquid. 'I didn't inject you. And in any case,' he added, '*Emu boomerangitis* is an emu virus, not a people virus.'

89   Wait and see

Half an hour later they had injected all eight young emus with the new virus.

'Now what?' said Brittany, who had removed her roller-buckets and was resting on her bed in the middle of a sea of whirling ceiling fans.

'Now,' Augustus said, 'we wait and see what happens.'

90   Get the police!

'Brittany, wake up!' her father whispered.

Brittany opened her eyes and yawned. She felt a bit light-headed but she was no longer dizzy. In fact, it was a long time since she had felt so *un*-dizzy. She looked at her watch. 'Huh?' she thought groggily. 'Only one watch – where have the other two gone?' Her single remaining watch said 2.24 p.m. She had been asleep for nearly an hour.

'What's going on?'

Her father, directly below her, pointed with his huge plaster cast. 'That's what's going on.'

Ernest, Evangeline, Engelbert, Elizabeth, Edward, Elly, Estha and Eggy were all crowded round the door trying to get out.

'What's the matter with them?'

'They want to go home,' Augustus said, sounding very pleased with himself.

He picked up the telephone beside his bed.

'Get me the police,' he said.

91   Homing emus

It was one of the weirdest sights ever seen on television.[38] A small dark-haired girl wearing roller-buckets on her feet, with a red bantam hen perched on her shoulder like a parrot, was being towed through the centre of Sydilly by eight half-grown emus. Surrounding them – four in front, two behind, each with its blue lights flashing and sirens wailing – was an escort of six police motorcycles.

Augustus watched the special live broadcast from his hospital bed. It lasted for nearly an hour. When the strange procession finally arrived at a familiar-looking house in a familiar-looking street, and was greeted by his wife and son and his grinning next-door neighbour (whose sleeveless denim jacket and jeans looked freshly washed), the scientist clenched his hands above his head in victory.

'It works!' he cried triumphantly. 'They found their way home!'

He had invented homing emus.

92   Wombats?

Next day – finally! – Brittany was on the front page of the newspaper.

There was a picture of her being towed down Georgina Street by Ernest, Evangeline, Engelbert, Elizabeth, Edward,

---

[38] But an even weirder one is coming later in the book.

Elly, Estha and Eggy. The photo showed Brittany, but the accompanying story was all about her father.

HU GETS JUMP ON WOMBATS

Street-birds everywhere received their marching orders yesterday when illustrious[39] CSIRO scientist, Dr Augustus Hu, released his brilliant new virus, *Emu boomerangitis*, in the Sydilly CBD.

Seen here being road-tested by Hu's daughter, the virus should ensure that the Olympic City is emu-free by the Opening Ceremony.

The new virus is a strain of *Iris boomerangitis*, which gives pigeons their powerful homing instincts. Once contracted, *E. boomerangitis* should cause all the street-birds to return to their places of birth.

"It's highly contagious," Hu said. "Every Australian city should be free of street-birds within a matter of weeks."

The Prime Minister described the new virus as a breakthrough. "This could be the most important Australian invention since the Wombat-jump plough," he said jubilantly.

No wombats were available to comment.

[39] A good word to describe your favourite author.

93   Don't know what I want

Brittany pushed the newspaper away from her in disgust. '"Hu's daughter"! They don't even say my name.'

'But it's a very nice photo of you,' Joanna said.

'It's awful! My pigtails are sticking straight up.'

Lukas examined the picture. 'You look like the Easter Bunny.'

'Do you want to wear the rest of my breakfast?' Brittany threatened.

'Not really. But I wouldn't mind the rest of your bacon, if you aren't going to eat it.'

Brittany slid the remains of her breakfast in her brother's direction.

'Are you sure you feel up to going to school today?' their mother asked.

'Now that you mention it,' Lukas said, busily loading Brittany's leftovers onto his own plate, 'I might just take the day off.'

The other two ignored him. Brittany said, 'I'm feeling fine, Mum.'

It was true. Even though she was flangling upside up at the breakfast bar with her feet firmly anchored in her roller-buckets, she wasn't even dizzy.

'How's your vision?' asked Joanna.

'20/20/20/20/20/20.'

'Oh dear!'

'Just joking,' Brittany grinned. 'Everything's A-okay, Mum. Truly.'

Joanna nodded. 'Well, as long as you're absolutely sure.'

'I *am* sure! I want to go back to school, I want to see my friends, I want to be...' Suddenly Brittany was blinking back tears. 'I just want everything to go back to normal!'

'I thought you wanted to be famous,' Lukas said with his mouth full.

'I do. I mean, I did.' Brittany shrugged. 'I guess I don't know *what* I want any more.'

94   Oops again

Augustus was released from hospital three days later. The whole family, as well as Mr Rankin from next door, celebrated his homecoming with a big feast of McKlucky Fried Chicken, which they ate out on the Hus' back patio because it was such a beautiful evening (and also because the emus weren't allowed inside). Marie Curie got a Vegetarian Pack[40], and for the emus there were eight[41] Fruit, Leaves and Insects Boxes. Meggs and Ginger hid under the house.

'Here's to the returning hero!' said Mr Rankin, raising his glass of orange fizz in a toast.

'To Dad!' everyone said. (Well, not *everyone* – there were a number of To Augustuses and Woofs and Booms[42] and Coos, and some rather loud trumpeting[43] as well.)

Augustus, propped up in his wheelchair with his plastered leg projecting forward like a huge, white battering ram, beamed in pleasure.

'It's very kind of you all,' he said modestly, giving Marie Curie's big saggy head a pat. 'But I would hardly call myself a hero.'

'Everyone else is,' Joanna pointed out.

'Even the Prime Minister!' added Lukas.

---

[40] Since Ernest, Evangeline, Engelbert, Elizabeth, Edward, Elly, Estha and Eggy had joined the family, Marie Curie refused to eat chicken.

[41] In case you're wondering what happened to Erica, she was last seen chasing a cyclist in Chapter 59.

[42] Emu-speak for 'What are we celebrating anyway?'

[43] Has anyone lost an elephant?

At that moment (their timing could not have been better), three men wearing pinstriped suits marched importantly round the side of the house. Pinstripe Number One came forward and shook Augustus's hand. At the end of the handshake, he gave a little frown, looked down at his own hand, removed a pinstriped handkerchief from his pocket and carefully wiped his fingers. Then he made a long speech.

Speeches – especially long ones – can be boring (this one was) so I won't write it down. But at the end of it, Number One opened his briefcase and, with a flourish that reminded some of those watching of a magician pulling a white rabbit out of a hat (others hoped for a white witchetty grub), he produced a large, official-looking certificate. It said:

Awarded to
Dr Augustus Hu
for Outstanding Service
to the Nation

It was signed by the Prime Minister, the Governor General, the Leader of the Opposition, the mayors of 24 coastal towns and cities, Mrs Tessa Brownfield[44] and the Captain of the Australian Cricket Team.

'...and so I would like to present you with this Certificate,' Number One finished his speech, 'on behalf of everybody.'

There was a long, awkward silence, which lasted until Joanna nudged Augustus with her elbow. His head jerked up.

'Th-thank you very much,' he stammered, accepting the certificate and blinking at it with a sleepy-eyed, pleased expression. 'Um, who's Mrs Tessa Brownfield?'

'I've got no idea,' said Number One. 'I think there's a footnote about it.'

---

[44] She was the tea lady in the Department for Generating Important Certificates.

Brittany roller-bucketed around to their three pinstriped visitors. 'Would you gentlemen like some chicken?'

'We're not allowed to eat on the job.'

'We're not allowed to eat on the job.'

'Yes please,' said Number One.

Afterwards, when all the chicken was gone[45] and so were all the visitors except Mr Rankin, Joanna stood behind Augustus's wheelchair and read the certificate over his shoulder.

'See!' she said. 'You *are* a hero!'

'Ahem!' said a stern and extremely official-sounding voice.

It was the three pinstriped men. They were standing at the corner of the house. Their pinstripes looked ruffled and so did their faces.

'Is something the matter?' Augustus asked.

Number One nodded his head. 'We can't get to our car.'

'Why ever not?'

'Come and see.'

Everyone trooped (and rolled) round the side of the house. And stopped dead.[46] What greeted them was the most amazing sight. Crowded on the front lawn, crammed into the driveway, gathered on the nature strip, swarming along the footpaths, circling overhead, perched on powerlines, letter-boxes, birdbaths, fences, trees, bent TV aerials, parked cars (including a pinstriped Holden Bureaucrat splattered with emu dung), neighbours' roofs and filling the entire street was the biggest flock of emus ever assembled in one place at one time.[47]

---

[45] Except Ginger and Meggs, who were still hiding.

[46] That's an exaggeration. The only one that stopped dead was a ladybug who had the misfortune to stop in the exact same place as one of Number One's Size 11 shoes.

[47] See the *McGuinness Book of Records*, under 'H' for Humungous herds, flocks, mobs and gaggles.

'Oops,' said Augustus, who had just worked something out.

95   Augustus explains (or tries to)

Here's what had happened.

Emus and pigeons aren't the same (have you noticed?) and even though *Emu boomerangitis* was nearly identical to *Iris boomerangitis*, its effect on emus wasn't the same as Iris's virus was on pigeons. The reason for this has something to do with the difference between emu DNA and pigeon DNA, and is much too complicated to explain here. Augustus tried to explain it and everyone fell asleep.

'The important thing to understand,' he said (when they had all woken up again), 'is that the pigeon virus causes all pigeons to return to their *own* homes, whereas the emu virus causes all emus to return to *Iris's* home.'

Brittany, who had taken off her roller-buckets when everyone came inside, peered upside down through the curtains. Everyone, including Mr Rankin and the three pinstriped men, was crowded into the Hus' living room because the whole house was surrounded. 'So why aren't they next door?' she asked.

'Iris lives here now,' explained her father. 'In our back shed.'

Mr Rankin scratched his stubbly head. 'What if we take Iris away?'

'It won't make any difference,' Augustus said. 'It's her home, not Iris, they're attracted to.'

There was the sound of a television news helicopter flying low overhead. Lukas rushed to the window and waved.

'It's a disaster!' said Number One. He had just been on

the phone to someone called Sir. 'The whole city is choked with street-birds! Every emu in the country is heading for Sydilly!'

'The Olympics are only three days away,' said Pinstripe Number Two.

'It's time to call in the Army!' said Number Three.

'Not the Army,' Brittany said. 'The Air Force.'

Everyone looked up at her.

96 How Brittany's dad's back shed ended up beyond the back of Bourke

'How big is the biggest Air Force helicopter?' asked Brittany.

Number One started to stretch out his arms, then realised they weren't long enough. 'Very big,' he said.

'Big enough to lift a shed?'

'It depends how big the shed is.'

Brittany crossed the ceiling and pointed out the back window. 'That big.'

'Not a problem,' said Number One, reaching for his mobile phone.

'Wait a minute!' Augustus objected. 'What are you intending to do with my back shed?'

'Turn it into an *out*back shed!' said Brittany.

In case you haven't worked out what it was yet, Brittany's plan was simple. The emus thought Augustus's shed was their home,[48] so why not move the shed off into the outback where they came from?

'Because my pigeons are in it!'

---

[48] Actually, they thought it was Iris's home, but *Emu boomerangitis* made them think Iris's home was their home. (If *you're* confused, think how the emus must have felt.)

'Your pigeons won't come to any harm, Mr Rankin,' Number One reassured him. 'We'll make sure they are well looked after. *And* you'll get a certificate like Mr Hu's,' he added.

'Signed by the Prime Minister, the Governor General, the Leader of the Opposition, the mayors of 24 coastal towns and cities, Mrs Tessa Brownfield and the Captain of the Australian Cricket Team?'

'Certainly.'

A crafty look crossed Mr Rankin's face. 'I'm actually more fond of tennis than I am of cricket.'

'So you'd prefer the Davis Cup captain to the cricket captain?' asked Number One.

Mr Rankin nodded. 'And maybe Kylie Minogue instead of one of the mayors?'

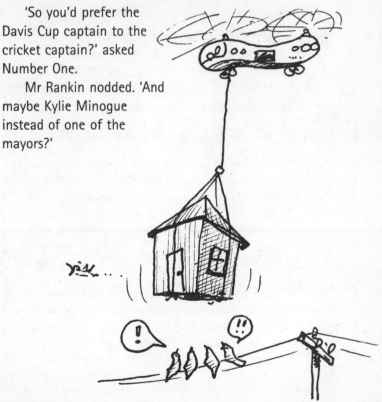

The helicopter – a huge, brown and green one with two enormous rotors – arrived 45 minutes later. Hovering noisily overhead, it lowered four steel cables with big hooks on the ends. Mr Rankin and the three pinstriped men attached the hooks to the four corners of the shed. Then the huge helicopter hoisted Augustus's shed up into the sky and whisked it off in the direction of the outback.

The emus, however, stayed put.

'I don't understand it,' Augustus said, peering out the window at the forest of street-birds all staring straight at the house. 'They should have followed the shed!'

97   I've called in the Army

Next morning Augustus was in the newspaper again.

BUNGLING BOFFIN BAFFLED

Fatuous[49] CSIRO scientist, Dr Augustus Hu, admitted last night that he has no idea why an estimated ten million emus have surrounded his Sydilly home.

Affected by the highly contagious new virus, *Emu boomerangitis*, the street-birds should be vamoosing to the outback, the doctor said.

Instead, they are converging on the Olympic City from all directions.

"It's a disaster!" Sydilly's mayor, Cr Ruth Marpole, said yesterday. "The entire city is in gridlock. Traffic can't move. Planes can't land. We'll have to cancel the Olympic Games!"

The Prime Minister, however, assures Olympic fans around the world that the Games, due to begin in two days time, will go ahead.

[49] Clue: it's got nothing to do with a person's shape.

"I've called in the Army," he announced at a special press conference last night.

Starting at first light tomorrow, 100,000 heavily armed soldiers will begin a massive street-bird eradication program in Sydilly's streets. For their own safety, the public are advised to stay indoors.

98   A serious chapter

Brittany stood near her bedroom window looking out. Two tears trickled down into her hair.

'It's horrible! What have the emus done?'

'Nothing,' said Joanna, standing directly below her. Her eyes were a bit wet too. 'But the situation is out of hand.'

Brittany leaned her forehead against the glass. A thousand emus were looking straight at her. 'GO AWAY!' she shouted angrily. 'THEY'RE GOING TO SHOOT YOU IF YOU DON'T GO AWAY!'

She felt her mother's hand stroking her hair. 'Come away from the window, Brit. There's nothing you can do.'

'There must be *something*! We could try chasing them.'

'It wouldn't do any good,' Joanna said. 'There are too many. And anyway, they would come straight back.'

Brittany knew her mother was right. There must have been 10,000 emus in their street alone. And it was like that throughout the city.

'It's all Dad's fault.'

'Don't say that, Brit.'

'But it is! If he hadn't invented that dumb toad virus in the first place, the Army wouldn't be going to shoot all the emus tomorrow.'

'You're right,' a voice said behind them. 'May I come in?'

It was her father. He must have heard everything Brittany had said. She didn't care. 'If you want to.'

Augustus came rolling into the room in his wheelchair. 'You're right about it being my fault, Brittany,' he said in a sad, tired-sounding voice. 'I thought it was a good idea but I wasn't careful enough. When the toad virus crossed over to the birds, things got out of control.'

'You weren't to know what would happen,' said Joanna.

'True. But I should have looked ahead, tried to foresee the possibilities.' Augustus made eye contact with his upside-down daughter. 'Sometimes we want something so much that we become blind to everything else.'

Brittany nodded. The same thing had happened to her. She had wanted to become famous and now here she was stuck on the ceiling for the rest of her life.[50]

'At least what *I* did won't cause ten million emus to be killed!'

Augustus gave her a weird, half-grin. 'In a way, your being de-gravitised *has* contributed to what's going on outside.'

99   A whole new virus

'What do you mean, *I* contributed?' Brittany asked crossly. 'You're the one who invented the stupid *Emu boomerangitis* virus that made all the emus come to Sydilly!'

Augustus wheeled further into the room. For the first time Brittany noticed a small microscope on his lap. 'I invented the virus,' he said, 'but I was working with an assistant, remember? And she had an accident as a result of her being de-gravitised, and *that* resulted in her being pricked by a syringe.'

[50] Okay, it wasn't for the rest of her life. But to an upside-down person seven years *seems* like a lifetime.

'What are you getting at, Dad?'

'When the needle pricked you, it became contaminated with your de-gravitised blood. That had a strange effect on what was inside the syringe – it changed it into a whole new virus.'

Brittany frowned. 'What sort of virus, exactly?'

100 An experiment

Augustus was conducting an experiment. When he had everything set up, he wheeled back through the house to the laundry door. Lukas was waiting for him.

'Now, Dad?'

Augustus nodded. 'Let them in, Lukey.'

101 What happened when Lukey let them in

Tickitty tickitty tickitty tickitty tickitty tickitty…SL-I-I-I-I-I-I-I-I-DE! 'Look out!' 'Yelp!' Shriek! Crash! Tinkle! Tickitty tickitty tickitty tickitty tickitty tickitty tickitty…[51]

102 Not homing emus

'Well!' said Number Two (or was it Number Three?), helping Joanna pick up little pieces of David. 'Where were they off to in such a hurry?'

Augustus, who had been spun round three times by the

---

[51] The sound made by eight little emus stampeding from one end of a house to another, and bowling over several people, one Saint Bernard dog, a rubber plant and a statue of Michelangelo's David along the way.

stampede, was looking dizzy but pleased with himself. 'Come and I'll show you.'

Everyone followed the path of destruction down to the end bedroom, where they found the eight little emus leaping up against the wardrobe doors as if they wanted to get inside.

'You can come out now,' Augustus called.

The top door popped open and Brittany stepped out onto the ceiling.

'Ta dah!' said Augustus.

Nearly everyone looked puzzled.

'What's this all about, Dr Hu?' asked Number One, brushing rubber-plant soil from his pinstripes.

Augustus pointed at Ernest, Evangeline, Engelbert, Edward, Elly, Estha and Eggy. 'How do you think they were able to find Brittany so quickly?'

'Because she smells?' Lukas suggested.

'I do *not* smell!' said Brittany. 'It's because of the virus.'

'What virus?' asked Mr Rankin.

'*Emu brittanitis*,' Augustus said. He rolled over to the window and pulled open the curtains. 'All those emus have got it.'

'I thought they had *Emu boomerangitis*.'

'So did I,' admitted Augustus, 'but I was wrong. They aren't homing emus, they're Brittanying emus.'

'You mean...?' said Joanna.

Augustus nodded. 'They're here because of Brittany.'

103 You look like Mick Doohan

'There's something I don't get,' Brittany said as her mother stood at the top of the stepladder helping her into Augustus's humungous Size 105 ski jacket. 'If they didn't have *Emu boomerangitis*, why did Ernest, Evangeline, Engelbert, Elizabeth, Edward, Elly, Estha and Eggy come home from the hospital?'

Augustus fiddled with the buckles of Mr Rankin's spare crash helmet. 'I knew someone was going to ask that,' he said. 'It's because they were hungry. We were so busy doing our experiments that we forgot to feed them.'

'Oh, Gus!' said Joanna.

He looked contrite. 'Well, it was only for half a day.'

Brittany stood still while her mother folded back the cuffs of the jacket's way-too-long sleeves. 'But how did they find their way home?'

'You had a police escort, remember,' her father said, passing the crash helmet up to Joanna, who pekuold[52] it on Brittany's head. 'I had already told them where we lived, so I guess Ernest and Co. simply followed them.'

Joanna strapped the crash helmet onto her daughter's head. 'There!' she said. 'You look like Mick Doohan.'

'I *feel* like an eskimo. Why do I have to wear all this stuff?'

'In case you fall off.'

'If I fall off, I'll fall up,' Brittany said, and just for a moment she had another of her dizzy spells. Then it was gone and she felt okay again.

'Here comes Mr Rankin!' Lukas called from the front room.

From outside came the sound of an approaching motorbike.

104 It might just work!

They tied Brittany's feet to the foot-pegs of Mr Rankin's huge silver Harley Davidson so she wouldn't llaf off.

---

[52] 'Plonked' upside down.

'All set?' asked Mr Rankin.

'All set!' said Brittany.

'Remember,' Augustus told Mr Rankin, 'emus can only go 40 kilometres per hour.'

'Phone us when you get there,' said Joanna.

'Don't forget to write!' joked Lukas.

'They're leaving now, Sir,' Number One shouted into his mobile phone. (He had to shout because a whole flock of news helicopters was hovering 200 metres overhead.) 'No, Sir, don't send in the Army just yet. As crazy as the idea sounds, I think it might just work!'

Brittany gave everyone the thumbs up. Then, closely followed by Ernest, Evangeline, Engelbert, Elizabeth, Edward, Elly, Estha and Eggy, the big, silver motorbike chugged slowly out of the Hus' carport and disappeared into the crowd of waiting emus.

105 Procession

The President of the Universal Olympics Corporation and his entourage were flying into Sydilly aboard a donated jumbo jet.

'Upon my word!' he suddenly exclaimed, pointing. 'What is that?'

Everyone with a window seat (and some rather rude people without) peered down.

'It appears to be some kind of procession, Mr President,' ventured one of his aides. 'Undoubtedly it is being staged in your honour.'

The President beamed with pleasure. 'A more glorious procession never in all my life have I laid on my eyes! Truly to be most heartily congratulated are the splendid citizens of Sydney.'

The aide coughed. 'Ahem, Mr President – it's Sydilly, not Sydney.'

106 Legend!

Lukas and Marie Curie lay sprawled on the floor in front of the television. Meggs was perched on the windowsill, her beak pressed against the flywire.

'Awesome!' muttered Lukas.

On TV there was an aerial shot of Sydilly. It showed a line of emus eighty or ninety birds wide that stretched from the city centre right out into the suburbs and then disappeared off the edge of the screen. All the emus were on the move, marching out of the city. The camera, which was obviously in a helicopter, followed the line of birds out into the country. Moving like a slow, brown river, the procession flowed along the main highway leading inland. At every intersection, police cars with flashing lights were stopping cars and trucks from entering the highway – there was only room for the emus. The procession went on and on. Across the coastal plains, up over the mountains, through forests, into the green and then brown hinterland. It seemed it was never going to end.

And then it did. Suddenly the helicopter reached the head of the procession and zoomed down for a closer look.

'Yaaay Brittany!' said Lukas.

Marie Curie and Meggs clucked and whimpered[53] in recognition.

Leading the ten million marching emus were Mr Rankin and Brittany on Mr Rankin's Harley Davidson. Right behind them came Ernest, Evangeline, Engelbert, Elizabeth, Edward, Elly, Estha, Eggy and then an adult emu that Lukas thought

---

[53] You sort it out.

could be Erica (he had one chance in ten million of being right). Suddenly Brittany grinned straight at the camera and gave a thumbs up.

Lukas stroked Marie Curie between her shoulder blades. 'My sister is a legend!' he said proudly.

107 Not just a legend

She wasn't just a legend, she was famous.[54]

108 Birdsville

Three days later the dusty Harley Davidson stopped outside a tiny outback town.

'Is this far enough?' Mr Rankin asked.

Brittany was feeling dizzy again. She wiped the dirt off her goggles and looked up at the sign.

BIRDSVILLE

'I guess so.'

Mr Rankin pulled his gloves back on. 'Good. Let's go home then.'

'We can't,' said Brittany.

'Why not?'

She pointed behind them. 'Because they'd follow us back to Sydilly.'

Mr Rankin contemplated the 50-metre-wide line of emus that stretched away across the desert for as far as the eye could see.

'They'd follow *you*,' he said craftily, 'not *me*.'

[54] At last!!!

It took Brittany a few moments to understand what he meant. 'You won't leave me here, will you, Mr Rankin?'

'Well, you just said you can't go back.'

Brittany surveyed the tiny town. 'I don't want to stay here on my own.'

'All right,' Mr Rankin said grumpily, 'I'll stay. But only until your mum or dad come to keep you company.'

He restarted the motorbike and roared down the main street towards a faded red sign that said 'Motel'.

109   Emusville

Next day there was a small article on page 42 of the Sydilly newspaper.

> ### EMUSVILLE
>
> The tiny outback town of Birdsville was invaded yesterday by an estimated 10 million emus.
>
> "It's a disaster!" said Birdsville's mayor, Councillor Benjamin Lord. "Our entire street is in gridlock! Livestock can't move, tumbleweed can't tumble!"
>
> If something isn't done soon, Councillor Lord said, the forthcoming Birdsville Cup race meeting will have to be cancelled.

110 Problems with being de-gravitised: Problem #18 – phone boxes

Brittany was standing upside down in a phone box surrounded by ten million emus. She felt a bit light-headed and her nose was blocked.[55]

'*When* can you get here?' she asked her mother.

'I don't know,' said Joanna. 'According to the newspaper, Birdsville is completely inaccessible at the moment. You sound a bit sniffly – are you okay?'

'Just a bit of a cold or something,' snivelled Brittany.

'Maybe you're allergic to emus.'

'It isn't funny, Mum!'

'Sorry,' Joanna said contritely. 'Maybe you should go and lie down, dear.'

'I don't want to lie down! I just want to go home,' wailed Brittany. On top of her cold or whatever it was, she had a mega dose of homesickness. 'I miss you all so much.'

[55] Problem #19 – runny noses.

'You poor darling. I'll fly up just as soon as they can shoo all the emus off the Birdsville airport. At least...'

Brittany sneezed eight times.

'At least you have Mr Rankin there to keep you company,' Joanna finished.

'He's so boring! All he talks about is motorbikes and pigeons.'

'Maybe you could play cards or something.'

'You can't play cards when you're upside down.'[56]

'But you could play "I spy",' Joanna suggested.

'Yeah, I guess so.' Brittany sniffed. 'How long will I have to stay here, Mum?'

'Until your father invents a cure for the emus so they won't follow you back.'

'Is he working on it?'

'Half an hour ago he was outside looking for stink bugs.'

'*Stink bugs?*'

'He has a theory about developing an emu repellant that you could spray on to make you unattractive to them.'

Brittany screwed up her nose. 'No way am I going to smell like a stink bug! Can I talk to him?'

'He isn't here at the moment. He had to pop down to the Olympics to receive a gold medal.'

'I beg your pardon?!!!' gasped Brittany.

111 Good on ya, Gus!

It was on the front page of the following day's newspaper.

---

[56] Problem #20 – playing cards.

GUS GETS GOLD

CSIRO genius, Dr "Gus" Hu, has won gold for Australia in the Sydilly Olympics.

Gus is seen here receiving his medal from the President of the UOC at a special ceremony yesterday.

The solid gold medal was awarded to Dr Hu for organising the best ever Olympics Parade in living (or dead) memory.

"I couldn't have done it without my family," said Gus, whose new wonder virus, *Emu brittanitis*, last week put an end to the nation's embarrassing street-bird problem.

112 I spy with my itchy eye

Brittany sneezed fourteen times, then blew her nose. Her eyes were sore. She felt dizzy and colicky and her homesickness was getting worse every day.[57] She and Mr Rankin were playing 'I spy' in the Guests' Lounge of the Birdsville Motel. They had been staying there for nearly a week and both of them were bored to tears (which might have been why Brittany's eyes were pink and wet)[58].

'I spy with my little eye something beginning with "e",' Mr Rankin said.

'Emu,' sniffed Brittany.

Mr Rankin nodded wearily.

---

[57] If there was a way to measure homesickness, Brittany could have gone in the *McGuinness Book of Records* for having the worst case of it ever recorded.

[58] But it wasn't.

'I spy,' Brittany said, 'with my rather itchy eye... something beginning with... "E".'

'Emu.'

'It's a capital E.'

'Ernest?'

'No.'

'Evangeline?'

'No.'

'Engelbert?'

'Yep.'

Mr Rankin gazed out the window. 'I spy with my little eye something beginning with... "E".'

'Emu.'

'Nope. It's a capital.'

Brittany went through all the emus' names she knew but Mr Rankin kept shaking his head. 'Is it Erica?' she tried finally.

'Nope,' he said, looking pleased with himself.

'Who is it then?'

'Do you give up?'

Brittany sighed. 'All right, I give up.'

'Ebeneeza.'

'Hey, that's cheating! There isn't one called Ebeneeza.'

Mr Rankin pointed. 'It's the fourth one from the right.'

'How do you know it's Ebeneeza?'

''Cos I just named it.'

'You can't do that, Mr Rankin. It makes it too hard.'

'All right. Your turn then.'

Brittany looked out the window. Because she was up on the ceiling she had a different view to Mr Rankin. 'I spy with my weepy eye something beginning with "I".'

'I?' he said, rubbing his tattoo. 'That's a hard one.'

Brittany wiped away a tear. 'It's a bird's name.'

'Now hang on a minute!' Mr Rankin objected. 'You just said we aren't allowed to make names up.'

'*I* didn't make it up – *you* did.'

'What are talking about?'

'Take a look,' Brittany said, pointing.

Mr Rankin stood up and saw what was perched on the windowsill.

'Iris!' he cried.

113   Pidge again

The motel manager led Mr Rankin around the back of the building. (Brittany stayed inside – she went back to her room to lie up.) 'There it is,' he pointed.

Sitting in the otherwise empty yard, with all Mr Rankin's pigeons perched along the roof, was Augustus's back shed!

'How did it get here?'

'A very big helicopter delivered it last week. We had no idea where it came from or what we were supposed to do with it. But I must say I've become rather fond of the little chaps,' the manager said, giving Iris a friendly scratch between her wings. 'Especially Pidge, here.'

'Her name isn't Pidge,' Mr Rankin said haughtily. 'It's Iris.'

114   Coming down with something

'I think I'm coming down with something,' Brittany said after dinner that night. 'I might go to bed early.'

Leaving Mr Rankin and the motel manager discussing pigeons, she went back to her room. As she stood upside down in front of the mirror brushing her teeth, she noticed something odd. Her hair was on end! Both pigtails were poking straight down towards the floor.

'Huh?' she said to her pasty-faced reflection. She felt too sick to worry about it. The room was spinning, her eyes were sore and, even though she had hardly touched her dinner, she felt like throwing down.

'I want to go home,' she whimpered.

Quickly finishing her teeth, Brittany stumbled across the ceiling to her bed (a mattress glued to the ceiling), collapsed on bottom of it and llafed immediately into a deep sleep.

115   Bump in the night

Zzzzzzzzzzzzzzzzzzz

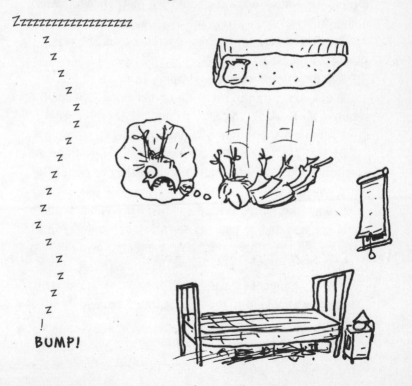

z
 z
  z
   z
    z
     z
      z
       z
        z
         z
          z
           z
            z
             z
              z
               !
BUMP!

At first Brittany thought she was dreaming. It was daylight.
The sun was streaming in through the window right into her
face. She squinted her eyes and blinked them a few times.
They weren't sore any more. In fact, all of her felt good. Her
nose didn't seem to be blocked. Her stomach felt fine. The
room wasn't spinning. She didn't even feel particularly
homesick!

Shading her eyes, Brittany peered at the window. That
was weird – she could see the sky. Usually when she lay in
bed and looked out the window all she could see was the
ground. Or emus. Today she could see neither. What was
going on?

Brittany slowly sat up. Yes, *up*, not *down*. She was
sitting on the floor!

'I'm gravitised!' she cried, leaping to her feet.

There was a frantic knocking on her door. 'Brittany!'
shouted Mr Rankin's voice. 'Wake up!'

'I am awake,' she said, letting him in.

At first Mr Rankin didn't notice she was upside up, he
was too excited about something else. 'They've gone! The
emus have gone!'

It was true. When Brittany went to the window all she
could see was one or two emus grazing contentedly in the
distance. All the others must have wandered away during
the night.

'What's happened?' she asked.

There was a loud roar as Flight OZ1 from Sydilly to
Birdsville flew low overhead.

'I've got no idea,' said Mr Rankin.

117   Back in the laboratory

Augustus peered into his electro-gravitoscope, where he had just recorded a number of electrographs of Brittany's brainwaves.

'Aha!' he said. 'Exactly as I thought.'

'What is it?' asked Brittany.

'When you were jabbed with the needle, you contracted a very mild dose of the emu virus. So mild, in fact, that it took nearly two weeks to affect you.'

'Is that why I was so homesick?'

Her father nodded. 'And why you experienced flu-like symptoms. But the most significant side effect is what happened to your body cells – they became re-gravitised.'

Brittany looked down at her feet, which were both planted solidly on the floor. She still wasn't used to it. 'And the emus?' she said. 'Why did they stop following me?'

'Because you caught the virus in reverse.' Augustus motioned her over to look into the electro-gravitoscope. 'You see, the virus affects the way the brain reacts to the earth's magnetic field, which in your case was the exact opposite to the way a normal gravitised brain worked. So instead of catching *Emu brittanitis*, you caught *Emu vamoosis*!'

All Brittany could see in the lens was a whole lot of wiggly lines. Which was exactly how her brain *felt*!

'Dad, I'm totally confused!'

'It is a bit complicated,' Augustus agreed. He picked up a little whiteboard and began writing on it. 'Maybe we should start at the beginning...'

Bufo lemmingitis + cane toads = Bye bye cane toads!   ✓
Bufo lemmingitis + emus = Oops!   ✗
Operation emu = Street-birds = Double oops!   ✗✗
Iris boomerangitis + pigeons = Homing pigeons   ✓
Emu boomerangitis + emus = Homing emus   ✓

BUT…

Contaminated Emu boomerangitis = Emu brittanitis   (!)
Emu brittanitis + emus = Brittanying emus   (!!)
Emu brittanitis + Brittany + de-gravitisation = Emu vamoosis   ✓
Emu vamoosis + Brittany = Bye bye emus!   ✓✓✓

'Am I the last one?' Brittany said.

Augustus nodded.

She screwed up her nose. 'So instead of being attracted to me, now the emus are *unattracted* to me?'

'Not exactly.' Her father picked up his marker again.

Emu brittanitis + Emu vamoosis = Normal   ✓✓✓✓

'What does that mean?'

'The forwards virus and the backwards virus cancel each other out. Emus aren't attracted to you, nor are they unattracted to you. You're the same as the rest of us.'

'So I'm normal,' said Brittany. She felt a bit better. 'But I guess we'll never see Ernest, Evangeline, Engelbert, Elizabeth, Edward, Elly, Estha and Eggy again.'

Augustus put his arm around her. 'It's better this way, Brit. They'll be much happier living in the outback than they would in Sydilly.'

Brittany sighed. 'Poor Meggs is going to miss them.'

'Not necessarily,' her father said in an I-know-something-you-don't kind of voice. 'Have you been out to the chook house lately?'

118 Matilda, Mason, Mitch, Marigold, Mopsy, Mel Gibson, Malcolm and Mitsy

'They're so cute!' Brittany said, carefully lifting one of the fluffy yellow bantam chicks (it might have been Marigold) out of the nest.

'I'll show you something,' said Lukas, grinning mysteriously.

Watched by a very proud-looking Meggs and Ginger (and a worried-looking Marie Curie), he gently took tiny Marigold (or was it Mitsy?) from his sister, held it out at arm's length, and let it go!

'What are you...?' Joanna started to say. Then stopped.

Because Mitsy (or Mel Gibson) flapped its tiny, half-formed wings and shot three metres straight up into the air!

'Lukas,' Augustus said as sternly as he could manage, 'you're grounded!'

119 One last thing

There was a knock on the door. It was Sunday night and the Hu family was half way through dinner (toad-in-the-hole – Augustus's favourite).

'I'll get it,' Brittany said, pushing her chair back from the table.

A Scotsman wearing a kilt stood on the doorstep. 'My name is Guinness McGuinness the Third,' he introduced himself. 'I represent the *McGuinness Book of Records*. Does a Brittany Hu live here?'

'I'm Brittany.'

The Scotsman reached into his sporran[59]. 'Is this you?' he asked, showing her a photo of a girl flangling upside down on the end of a short piece of rope.

Brittany recognised it immediately. It was the photo someone took of her on the way home from the jetty the day they rescued Erica from the sea.

'I...I'm not sure,' she said.

Guinness McGuinness the Third scratched under his tam-o'-shanter[60]. 'If we could just verify who it was, we could enter her in the *McGuinness Book of Records* as the World's Lightest Person. She could be famous!'

Brittany handed the photo back. 'It couldn't be me, Mr McGuinness the Third – I weigh 38 kilos.'

After the Scotsman had gone, Brittany stood for a moment looking down at her new (Size 2) Doc Martens. She tapped one toe on the bare floorboards in a little rhythm: *tap tap tappity-tap*! Then she tried the other one: *tappity-tappity tap tap tap*! Then she tap-danced all the way back to the dining room.

Everyone was looking at her as she sat back down at the table.

'What?' said Brittany.

[59] Ask a Scotsman what this is. (And while you're about it, ask him about a tam-o'-shanter.)

[60] You should have already asked about this.

Augustus helped himself to more toad-in-the-hole. 'We heard what you said to Guinness McGuinness.'

'The Third,' Lukas added.

Marie Curie came over and put her head on Brittany's knee.

'Why didn't you tell him it was you?' asked Joanna.

Brittany smiled at her family. 'I guess I just like being normal.'

120 Another last thing

PIGEONVILLE

This year's famous Birdsville Cup race meeting, recently in danger of being cancelled, will go ahead as usual.

*Un*usual will be the form of racing involved. Race Organiser, Mr Seymour Rankin, said this year's event will feature pigeons rather than horses.

Rankin, a breeder of champion racing pigeons and founder of the newly formed Flying Emus Motorcycle Club, recently moved to Birdsville from Sydilly.

"This is a more wholesome environment for bringing up birds," he said. "Sydilly was too much of an emu race."

Asked for his tip for the Cup, Rankin said to keep an eye on Brittany's Dream. From the nest of celebrity pigeon Iris, Brittany's Dream has all the qualities of a future champion, Rankin said.

"One day she's going to be famous," he predicted.

121 Definitely the last last thing!

Nearly three thousand kilometres away, on the other side of the Tasman Sea, a little girl and her brother were collecting sea shells on a New Zealand beach.

'Look,' said the girl. 'A frog!'

An enormous, very tired-looking cane toad came hopping out of the waves.

'There's another one,' the boy pointed.

'And another!' shrieked the girl.

Soon the beach was covered with huge, brown, warty toads.

'Yuck! They're really gross.' The boy pulled a face as he and his sister backed away from the slowly advancing army of hopping, slithering *Bufo*s. 'Let's get out of here!'

As the two children raced away across the sand dunes, a small brown kiwi, New Zealand's famous flightless bird, emerged from a nearby band of rainforest and began pecking its way innocently down towards the shore.

Author's note: No emus were injured during the writing of this book. The ladybug stepped on in Chapter 94 (Footnote 46) made a full recovery and lived to a ripe old age of seven weeks. Augustus's broken leg was never quite the same again – when it healed it was twenty millimetres shorter than the other one and he went on to become the World Hopping Champion. (See the *McGuinness Book of Records*, under 'H' for *Hu*. There's a whole chapter about him.) Brittany, who now weighs 38.2 kilos, wrote a book about her adventures and published it under a false name.